STAR TREK®: THE KLINGON™ WAY—

A Warrior's Guide

STAR TREK®: THE KLINGON™ WAY—

A Warrior's Guide

tlhIngan tIgh: SuvwI' DevmeH paq

Compiled, translated, and annotated by

Marc Okrand

POCKET BOOKS
New York London Toronto Sydney Tokyo Singapore

An *original* Publication of POCKET BOOKS
POCKET BOOKS, a division of Simon & Schuster Inc.
1230 Avenue of the Americas, New York, NY 10020

ISBN: 0-671-53755-5

First Pocket Books trade paperback printing May 1996

10 9 8 7 6 5 4 3 2 1

Printed in the U.S.A.

Introduction

Until recently, the Klingon Empire and the United Federation of Planets had been at peace for some eighty years and allies for a quarter century. During that time, each society had come to know the other in ways neither could have imagined possible during the previous seventy or so years of antagonism. The Federation increased its knowledge of the Empire's history, politics, economics, and, to a lesser degree, language and traditions relatively early on. This led to a thriving economic relationship as well as unexpected cultural enrichment. All this, however, may have come to an end as a result of the Klingon withdrawal from the Khitomer Accords, the peace treaty between the Empire and the Federation, following Federation opposition to the Klingon invasion of the Cardassian Union.

Before the era of peace, most citizens of the Federation considered Klingons to be warlike, hostile, savage, primitive, rude, close minded, threatening, aggressive, ruthless, demanding, temperamental, brutal, and generally rather unpleasant. As Captain James T. Kirk once put it, "They're animals." Though increased interaction with the Klingons did not entirely disprove any of these characterizations, it did make it obvious that such descriptive terms are incomplete. Klingons, it was seen, are efficient, loyal, cunning, strong, proud, and, above all, honorable. Though some progress has been made, getting a firm grasp on the true nature of the Klingons—their basic character traits, their real values and guiding principles—remains elusive. The fact that the Klingon Empire's response to the political situation in the Cardassian Union took the Federation by surprise has only underscored the lack of real understanding.

In order to find out more about the Klingons, some in the Federation have insisted that it is necessary to get inside the Klingon mind: to see what Klingons believe, how they think, how they react naturally to situations. Federation social scientists used to argue that a lack of such knowledge would be a hindrance to making the alliance more solid, and inevitably lead to miscommunication followed by outbreaks of discord and distrust. Their predictions proved accurate.

With the goal of reestablishing peace with the Empire—or at least of being able to predict what the Klingons might do next—the Federation Scientific Research Council has launched an investigatory project to catalog Klingon beliefs about life and the universe. This is intended to supplement the Klingon cultural database that has been available for some time and has been used in conjunction with various Federation missions. As extensive as that database is, it often lacks the Klingons' own perspectives on their culture. Given the current political situation, it is difficult to ask Klingons questions, so the procedure has been to let Klingons speak for themselves—to listen to comments they have made to justify positions or to explain actions. By examining the Klingons' own words, their moral and ethical values should become apparent. This compilation is the project's initial report, bringing together statements that, directly or indirectly, illustrate Klingon virtues.

A "virtue" is a particularly valued quality or a form of behavior that exemplifies moral correctness, as defined by a society. Those members of Starfleet who have had the most contact with the Empire have noted that, in Captain Jean-Luc Picard's words, "The Klingons are efficient, loyal to their beliefs, and are regulated by a strict code of ethics." Indeed, the Klingon word "**ghob**" may be translated as "ethics" or "virtue," linguistic evidence that the concept is not unknown or never discussed among the Klingons themselves. It is probably significant that the Klingon word for "do battle," or "wage war" is likewise "**ghob.**"

Though some, perhaps many, of a society's virtues are represented in its legal codes, a virtue is not a law. A violation of a virtue need not carry with it any legal sanction. A virtue does not even have to be followed all the time to still be considered a virtue. What is important is that members of the society agree that the virtue represents what *should* be done, even if it is not done. When a virtue is ignored, all recognize the transgression, even if there are no immediate consequences.

A society's values are often encapsulated in its repertoire of proverbs or maxims, common statements of fundamental truths that are applicable to many situations. Such expressions are well known by the members of the society.

They are often short and are frequently (some might say too frequently) uttered. They give advice generally accepted to be worth heeding. The meaning of many proverbs is reasonably straightforward, such as the old Federation saw "Out of sight, out of mind," which suggests that anything or anyone not present is apt to be forgotten. In other cases, the meaning is metaphorical. "Too many cooks spoil the broth," for example, usually has nothing to do with preparing soup. Such phrases make reference to items or activities familiar in the culture—in this case, cooking—in order to make more general points. An interesting feature of proverbs is that, to some extent, they may contradict one another. In addition to "Out of sight, out of mind," one hears "Absence makes the heart grow fonder" (anything or anyone not present is thought about more positively, if not more frequently). Both proverbs are valid; a complex society may have multiple points of view.

Other phrases illustrating a society's values are not so common, not necessarily known by the population at large. Perhaps they are found in literary works known only to a certain subgroup. They may be related to a certain occupation or be heard in only one locality. Nonetheless, they still embody certain tenets shared by the society as a whole.

One problem that often arises is where to find these various statements. Simply asking someone to recite a list of proverbs is of limited utility; they are far better understood if heard in context, springing forth naturally in a particular situation. For Klingon utterances there is, fortunately, a huge databank that can be consulted for just such occurrences. For years, Starfleet has been keeping ships' and personal logs on file. The Research Council has been granted access to these archives for purposes of this study. Contained in these logs are numerous comments actually made by or attributed to Klingons encountered during various missions, including a large number uttered by the first Klingon to become a Starfleet officer, Lieutenant Commander Worf. In addition, the Council, as part of its ongoing linguistic research, has been collecting numerous Klingon phrases, many of which fall into the categories useful for the current study.

In this report, those sayings (or references to sayings) found in the Starfleet archives are so noted, identified by the nicknames Starfleet has given to various missions. An explanation of these identifications is found at the end of this report. Sayings without such annotations are taken from the linguistic studies. All phrases are given in both Federation Standard and Klingon, transcribed in the romanization system most commonly used in the Federation today. Even though many of these sayings were first recorded in Federation Standard, they tend to have fixed phrasings in Klingon. To determine what they are, Klingons have been consulted in each case, though this has not always been easy. By the same token, some of the sayings are not new to the Federation and have come to have standardized translations. Though commonly heard (and used in this report), these translations are not always the most revealing ones. For example, "**Dujeychugh jagh nIv yItuHQo'**" is translated, "There is nothing shameful in falling before a superior enemy"—a simple statement. A more literal translation, however, is "If a superior enemy defeats you, don't be ashamed," a direct command. Indeed, many Klingon proverbs are commands, a telling fact in its own right. As appropriate, additional notes about usage, background, or translation are provided for many phrases, though some are left to stand on their own.

This report is, of course, the result of a collaborative effort. A full team of researchers devoted a great deal of time to going through mission reports, conducting ancillary investigations, translating, and so on. Any benefit gained from this report is due to their hard work. Any errors or misinterpretations are the author's.

It is hoped that this report, which is really a collection of traditions and beliefs and virtues captured in speech, will make a contribution towards the appreciation of Klingon identity and pride and will help lead to the reconciliation of the two governments. **Qapla'**.

STAR TREK®: THE KLINGON™ WAY—

A Warrior's Guide

ROBBIE ROBINSON

A clone of Kahless (Kevin Conway) created with all the memories and values of the true Kahless.

We are Klingons!

tlhIngan maH!

This is the strongest expression of joy among Klingons and probably the most frequently heard Klingon phrase. It is used not only in the throes of battle but on any other joyous occasion as well. When Kahless the Unforgettable, who united the Klingon Empire, was cloned years later, the replica retained the ancient Klingon attitudes. He said to Gowron, the leader of the Klingon High Council, "You have no joy, Gowron. Is your heart so filled with distrust and suspicion that you have forgotten what it is to be truly Klingon?"

The Next Generation: Rightful Heir

ROBBIE ROBINSON

To extract the needed information, Worf (Michael Dorn) uses a Klingon approach.

**Klingons are born,
live as warriors, then die.**

bogh tlhInganpu', SuvwI'pu' moj, Hegh.

**Klingons are born
to fight and to conquer.**

SuvmeH 'ej charghmeH bogh tlhInganpu'.

These two maxims express the belief that fighting and winning define a Klingon's very being; everything else in life is secondary, if not superfluous. Unless they are engaged in battle or preparing for battle, Klingons become rather cantankerous (though, to those unfamiliar with Klingons, this might not be noticeable). As a result, Klingons are likely to, at the slightest provocation, instigate a battle of some sort.

Lieutenant Commander Worf is well aware of the Klingon predilection reflected in these two sayings. Though raised among humans, he has always prided himself on his knowledge of Klingon history and culture. He observed that a potentially dangerous situation involving the Dominion and the Cardassians, which the Klingons viewed as a threat, "has given my people an excuse to do what they were born to do: to fight and to conquer."

The Next Generation: Coming of Age
Deep Space Nine: The Way of the Warrior

ROBBIE ROBINSON

The son of Mogh confronts his own "lack of faith" with action.

When threatened, fight.

DabuQlu'DI' yISuv.

This is one of many common exhortations that encourage Klingons to respond to situations appropriately.

After the *Enterprise*'s initial encounter with the entity Q, Worf gave voice to this attitude. He advised Captain Jean-Luc Picard that "our only choice is to fight." If we Klingons understand anything, it is the meaning of that kind of talk.

The Next Generation: Encounter at Farpoint

We fight to enrich the spirit.

qa' wIje'meH maSuv.

A more literal translation of this Klingon phrase is "We fight in order to feed the spirit," focusing more on the role of the giver of enrichment (the Klingon) than that of the recipient (the spirit). For Klingons, the spirit is something that must be cared for actively. As the clone of Kahless pointed out, fighting is more than a physical activity: "We do not fight merely to spill blood, but to enrich the spirit." Interestingly, because of the homophony of the Klingon words for "feed" and "buy," both "**je'**," the phrase could also be translated as "We fight in order to buy the spirit." If this is not mere coincidence, then, perhaps, to the Klingon way of thinking, while one is alive, one must sacrifice or give up something (the way one uses credits or latinum when making a purchase) in order to ensure that the spirit is one's own.

The Next Generation: Rightful Heir

If you are sad, act!

bI'IQchugh yIvang!

This exhortation is actually ambiguous, but both interpretations give insight into the Klingon way of thinking. The phrase could be advising one to take specific action to overcome sadness—that is, figure out exactly what the problem is and do something about it. On the other hand, for a Klingon, activity and vigor are associated with a sense of elation, while unhappiness is often connected to passivity or even laziness, character traits disdained by Klingons. Thus, the advice could be simply to do anything at all.

Hit them hard and hit them fast.

tIqIpqu' 'ej nom tIqIp.

When the *Enterprise* was held in the grip of a Ferengi force field, Worf offered this advice to Captain Picard as a way to deal with the opponent. Once again, the importance of taking action, of not being passive or reticent, may be observed in the suggestion.

The Next Generation: The Last Outpost

Klingons do not procrastinate.

lumbe' tlhInganpu'.

Not only do Klingons see the virtue of taking action, they prefer to take action right away. From the Klingon point of view, although planning and organizing are appropriate, there is no reason not to proceed with any mission or task once the goal is established.

The Next Generation: Liaisons

If it's in your way, knock it down.

Dubotchugh yIpummoH.

Though split into two individuals—one fully Klingon, one fully human—by a Vidiian scientist, the human B'Elanna Torres still retained her Klingon knowledge, if not her Klingon impulses. She cited this adage—again illustrating the Klingon penchant for action and for taking control—when she commented on the behavior of her Klingon self.

Voyager: Faces

Gowron (Robert O'Reilly) clashes with his friend over how to survive as Klingons.

To survive, we must expand.

mataHmeH maSachnIS.

This has long been a rallying cry among Klingons. When Commander Kang and a group of stranded Klingons forced James T. Kirk into letting them board the *Enterprise* after their own ship had been destroyed, the Federation crew and the Klingons became engaged in a series of bloody skirmishes, with neither side able to achieve victory. Captain Kirk realized that an alien life form aboard the ship was controlling them, causing them to continue the fighting. The only way to thwart this entity was to work together with the Klingons and stop the hostilities. Kang's science officer and wife, Mara, did not think it would be easy to convince him to cooperate, since combat is the Klingon way. "We have always fought," she said. "We must . . . We must push outward if we are to survive."

Years later, the idea is still present in the Klingon consciousness. Worf once noted that many Klingons feel "the Empire must expand to survive." The word for "survive," "**taH**," can also be translated "continue, endure, go on."

The Original Series: Day of the Dove
Deep Space Nine: The Way of the Warrior

ROBBIE ROBINSON

Believing he has only one course of action, Gowron takes it.

Klingons are a proud race, and we intend to go on being proud.

Hem tlhIngan Segh 'ej maHemtaH 'e' wIHech.

The first formal meeting between the Klingon Empire and the United Federation of Planets, which eventually resulted in their alliance, was held on Khitomer, a planet near the Klingon-Romulan border. Representing the Empire was Azetbur, who was appointed to lead the Klingon High Council after her father, Chancellor Gorkon, was assassinated by a coalition of those opposed to the impending peace. In her address to the conference, Azetbur altered this saying slightly when she insisted that the treaty in no way diminished the stature of the Klingon Empire: "We are a proud race, and we are here because we intend to go on being proud."

Years later, as the Federation-Klingon alliance began to fall apart, Klingon leader Gowron still adhered to this virtue. When he discovered that his rationale for moving against the Federation was based on misinformation, he held his ground, maintaining Klingon pride by coming up with a new justification for his aggression. That the Dominion had not taken over the Cardassian government "is of no consequence," Gowron said. "All that matters is that the Alpha Quadrant will be safer with the Klingon Empire in control of Cardassia."

Star Trek VI: The Undiscovered Country
Deep Space Nine: The Way of the Warrior

ROBBIE ROBINSON

Huraga (William Dennis Hunt) raises voice and drink with his old friend's son.

Great deeds, great songs.

ta'mey Dun, bommey Dun.

Though the subtleties of Klingon music are not often appreciated by non-Klingons, songs are a very important part of Klingon culture, for it is through song that much history—both political and personal—is preserved. Great accomplishments are commonly immortalized in song, as are Klingon attitudes. Because songs are repeated, the same way proverbs are repeated, they help to preserve tradition as well as to teach the young. The singing of a song typically marks an occasion as momentous. Appropriately, Gowron tried to get Worf to join his cause by referring to this element of Klingon culture: "We will do great deeds in the coming days, deeds worthy of song." Klingons are also well known for their extensive collection of drinking songs.

Deep Space Nine: The Way of the Warrior

Trying to deny her Klingon heritage proves fruitless: K'Ehleyr (Suzie Plakson) shares the joy of battle with Worf.

The memory of you sings in my blood.

bomDI' 'IwwIj qaqaw.

This is a line excerpted from a Klingon poem. Poetry plays a prominent role in Klingon mating behavior. The female typically roars, throws heavy objects, and claws at her partner. The male reads love poetry and, as Worf put it, "ducks a lot." This particular line is interesting because it reinforces the importance of song as a memory-triggering device. The literal, though less poetic, translation of the line is "When my blood sings, I remember you." Presumably the blood's song concerns the beloved individual.

The Next Generation: The Dauphin
The Next Generation: Up the Long Ladder

ROBBIE ROBINSON

The protection of the ship and her crew is the security chief's prime concern. He knows that the Klingon way will serve them well.

Choose to fight, not negotiate.

bISuv 'e' yIwIv; bISutlh 'e' yIwIvQo'.

If you must negotiate, watch your enemy's eyes.

bISutlhnISchugh jaghlI' mInDu' tIbej.

While negotiation is not the Klingon's first choice of an approach to settling differences, it is not to be ruled out altogether. Worf himself has articulated the ideas embodied in both of these proverbs. Regarding the search for diplomatic solutions, he once remarked, "This is hopeless. Fighting would be preferable." On the other hand, when talk is called for, one must not rely on words alone: "I prefer to negotiate eye to eye with my enemy."

The Next Generation: The Ensigns of Command
The Next Generation: Evolution

Worf and his brother Kurn (Tony Todd) listen silently as the charges are read against their father.

Brute strength is not the most important asset in a fight.

Suvlu'taHvIS yapbe' HoS neH.

As vital as musculature and weaponry are in winning battles or maintaining control, other qualities are equally if not more important. The unstated significance of this maxim is that intelligence and judgment play key roles in any confrontation.

When Worf learned that his father, who had been killed by Romulans in the Khitomer massacre, was later falsely accused of treason, he decided to exercise his responsibility as a son and appear before the Klingon High Council either to clear his father's name or to be punished for his crimes. According to Klingon custom, even though Worf was the one bringing the challenge, he was considered the accused since he would bear the punishment if the accusations against his father stood. During the course of the proceedings he was not permitted to participate in any fights himself, but instead was defended by an aide ("**cha'DIch**," literally, "second").

After Kurn, Worf's younger brother and first **cha'DIch**, was wounded, Worf asked Captain Picard to be his **cha'DIch**. Though, as Picard pointed out, stronger men were available, Worf preferred the captain, undoubtedly because of his shrewdness and loyalty. Such qualities are valued more than physical prowess alone.

ROBBIE ROBINSON

His understanding of Klingon politics gives Worf the leverage needed to have Gowron proclaim the clone of Kahless as Emperor.

Real power is in the heart.

tIqDaq HoSna' tu'lu'.

In this phrase, the heart stands for one's spirit or principles. One's ability to exert influence over others comes from having a strong sense of morality, not merely from the ability to dominate by force.

When the clone of Kahless was named emperor, the Klingon cleric Koroth objected that it would be meaningless since all power would still remain with the Klingon High Council. Worf used this adage to point out that Kahless's lack of political authority was not as important as his honor and virtue, which would make him an effective leader of his people.

The Next Generation: Rightful Heir

There is nothing shameful in falling before a superior enemy.

Dujeychugh jagh nIv yItuHQo'.

The Next Generation: The Last Outpost

There is no honor in attacking the weak.

pujwI' HIvlu'chugh quvbe'lu'.

Though sometimes difficult to discern, it would appear that Klingons do have a sense of fair play. Worf quoted this aphorism to his son, Alexander, who had just bullied a group of children. Though phrased in presumably military terms, the ethic expressed by the saying runs throughout Klingon society.

The Next Generation: Reunion

When in doubt, surprise them.

bISovbejbe'DI' tImer.

This offering of wisdom is commonly understood as a suggested battle strategy. "When you are uncertain about what to do in a confrontation," it advises, "choose the course of action your opponent is least likely to be anticipating." This complements the following cited tenet. If one trusts one's instincts, even when full knowledge is lacking, one will be able to make a decision, pursue a course of action, and, therefore, catch one's opponent off guard. Once, when the *Enterprise* entered a black void and nothing seemed to work properly, Worf suggested adhering to this Klingon tactic as Commander William Riker and he prepared to beam onto the *U.S.S. Yamato*, just in case the Federation vessel was not as deserted as it appeared to be.

The Next Generation: Where Silence Has Lease

Korris (Vaughn Armstrong) tries to play on Worf's sympathies and sway him to his position.

Trust your instincts.

DujlIj yIvoq.

Klingon Commander Kruge invoked this principle when, after attacking the *Enterprise*, he concluded that the Federation starship may have suffered substantial damage. Though there was no concrete evidence of this, he said "I trust my instincts."

Similarly, Klingon renegades Korris and Konmel, beamed aboard the *Enterprise* just before their own (stolen) ship exploded, appealed to this notion when they tried to lure Worf to reject the Klingon-Federation alliance and join them. "Our instincts will lead us," said Korris. "Instincts that have not been dulled by living among 'civilized' men," Konmel added, by way of clarification.

The Klingon word for instincts is "**Duj**," and it is grammatically correct to treat it as singular (a bundle or collection of instincts) or plural (individual instincts). "**Duj**" also means "ship" or "vessel," so a possible interpretation of the aphorism is "trust your ship." In this context, a vessel could symbolize oneself. To a Klingon, this reveals a deep truth.

Star Trek III: The Search for Spock
The Next Generation: Heart of Glory

Challenged by an inferior officer, Commander Riker (Jonathan Frakes) reacts in time-tested Klingon fashion.

There are no old warriors.

SuvwI'pu' qan tu'lu'be'.

This does not mean that all warriors are young at heart. It is quite literal. Traditionally, if a captain becomes weak and incapable of serving, he is assassinated by his first officer. A similar arrangement is in effect for officers of lower rank. As Worf put it, "The Klingon system has operated successfully for centuries."

The Next Generation: A Matter of Honor

Alone in a ship of humans, the renegade Klingons Konmel (Charles H. Hyman) and Korris try to gain an ally.

Listen to the voice of your blood.

'IwlIj ghogh yIQoy.

For Klingons, blood is more than just one of a number of red-pink bodily fluids. It represents the animating force of life itself, that which controls basic temperament and character. It is strength. It is the commander, making the decisions and giving the orders. With effort, its influence can be repressed, but never entirely ignored. For a warrior to get in touch with himself, to lead a truly effective life, he must pay attention to, or listen to, what his blood has to say. Though Konmel used the common Federation Standard translation when he tried to get Worf to join him, the Klingon version of this frequently heard exhortation is a bit more pointed. The verb "**Qoy**" means "hear," not just "listen." One must actually perceive and understand that which is being said.

The Next Generation: Heart of Glory

A warrior's blood boils before the fire is hot.

tujpa' qul pub SuvwI' 'Iw.

This proverb suggests that it is better to take the initiative than to simply react to situations. Blood, the controller, does not need an external influence in order to heat up; one need not draw strength from the outside.

Perhaps because of increased association with the Federation, or perhaps simply as a result of the progression of time, the number of venues available to Klingons to act on their basic genetic need for battle and confrontation—their boiling blood—has diminished. Whereas once Klingon warriors would use the slightest provocation as justification for a fight, today, more so than in the past, the strengths and skills of the warrior are often demonstrated ritualistically. Mock battles and tournaments are staged, such as the competition on Forcas III, in which Klingons prove their skills at wielding the **bat'telh**, the traditional sword.

In space, all warriors are cold warriors.

loghDaq Suvrupbogh SuvwI'pu'
chaH Hoch SuvwI'pu''e'.

Since this expression refers to being in space **(loghDaq)**, it is either a relatively new saying or else it is an updated version of an older one. There is no way to know for sure. Klingons have been capable of interplanetary travel for at least 200 standard years, enough time for many new phrases to work their way into common usage. Clearly, it refers to warriors being in an environment far away from governmental or bureaucratic fetters, a setting where warriors are free to be just warriors and not worry about political consequences. Without knowing more about ancient Klingon history, what, if anything, might have predated "**loghDaq**" in the expression cannot be determined. Perhaps it was a term referring to the open seas, as the Klingons have a history of naval warfare. The Klingon words translated "cold warriors" are "**Suvrupbogh SuvwI'pu',**" literally, "warriors who are ready to fight."

Star Trek VI: The Undiscovered Country

Blood and water don't mix.

tay'taHbe' 'Iw bIQ je.

Just as "blood" is used figuratively to refer to power, "water" carries the opposite and negative connotation of lack of control. Strength cannot coexist with weakness within an individual or a successful society. Klingon scientist J'Ddan used "water" in this way when criticizing the influence the Federation had on the Empire: "The blood of all Klingons has become water."

The Next Generation: The Drumhead

One is always of his tribe.

reH tay' ghot tuqDaj je.

This is an old Klingon adage that years ago was rendered into Federation standard in the form cited, using the word "tribe" for "**tuq,**" an ancestral grouping now usually translated as "house." The literal meaning of the Klingon phrase is "A person and his house are always together." Though cast in terms of family, the expression can apply to friendship as well. The basic idea conveyed is that no matter what happens and no matter where one may go, one remains attached to family and significant friends.

Drinking fake ale is better than drinking water.

tlhutlhmeH HIq ngeb qaq law' bIQ qaq puS.

"Fake ale" is a term used to refer to a rather nonpotent ale, perhaps akin to "near beer." Again, the negative image of water—weakness—emerges. Anything is better than water; the less waterlike, the better. Therefore, it is not surprising that Worf commented that the prune juice served to him by Guinan is "a warrior's drink." It is not at all watery. The negative associations with water might also be seen when Worf remarked to Counselor Deanna Troi, "Swimming is too much like bathing."

The Next Generation: Yesterday's Enterprise
The Next Generation: Conspiracy

DANNY FELD

Three old comrades—Kor (John Colicos), Koloth (William Campbell), and Kang (Michael Ansara)—unite to take action against a deadly foe.

A warrior does not let a friend face danger alone.

nIteb Qob qaD jup ’e’ chaw’be’ SuvwI’.

The central issue addressed in this adage is loyalty. When Soren, a J’naii with whom Commander Riker fell in love, was arrested for exhibiting gender-specific feelings, a crime among the J’naii, Riker decided to act on his own and rescue her before she was forced to undergo therapy that would remove these feelings. Worf offered to help his friend, citing this Klingon virtue as his rationale. This was not the first time Worf exhibited this type of behavior. Before Riker boarded the *Pagh*, a Klingon ship on which he served in an officer exchange program, Worf gave him an emergency transponder. The commander could then be located and beamed back if necessary. Though Worf said it was simply a security precaution, both Riker and he knew it was an expression of friendship and loyalty. Worf would not permit Riker to face the potential danger alone.

Even though this Klingon character trait might be considered an admirable one, even by non-Klingons, it might not be all that selfless. If Riker had accepted the captaincy of the *Ares*, Worf would have joined him on that ship. The Klingon pointed out that it could have been a “dangerous mission” with “the potential for combat”. The underlying motivation for such altruism, it would appear, is that Klingons do not want to be left out if there is even the slightest possibility that there will be a battle.

The Next Generation: The Outcast
The Next Generation: A Matter of Honor
The Next Generation: The Icarus Factor

When a warrior goes to a battle, he does not abandon his friends.

may'Daq jaHDI' SuvwI' juppu'Daj lonbe'.

This might be a stronger statement about friendship and loyalty than the preceding adage, for here the admired virtue is to make sure that friends have the opportunity to participate in battle.

Three Klingon captains—Kang, Koloth, and Kor—were once ordered to stop a series of raids on Klingon colonies by a group of depredators led by an albino. Although their mission was successful, the albino escaped, promising to take revenge on the firstborn of each of the three captains. He did so by infecting the Klingon children with a fatal genetic virus. One of the children was the godson of Curzon Dax, a Federation diplomat. Dax was admired by the child's father, Kang—who had once had an encounter with Captain James T. Kirk—for his diplomatic accomplishments and his understanding of Klingon nature. The three Klingon captains, along with Curzon Dax, took a blood oath to find the albino and avenge the deaths of the children.

Curzon Dax was a Trill, a joined species consisting of a humanoid host and a symbiont that resides within the host. When Curzon, the trill host, was near death, the symbiont Dax was transplanted. The new host, Jadzia Dax, though considered another person, retains all of the memories of Curzon, as well as of previous joinings.

When the whereabouts of the albino were finally discovered, the three Klingon captains came together on space station Deep Space 9 to prepare to exact revenge. Jadzia Dax, the station's science officer, though technical-

DANNY FELD

Jadzia Dax (Terry Farrell) works with her friend Kang to overcome insurmountable odds.

ly not bound by Curzon's oath, wanted to honor it. Kang withheld his approval until Jadzia, drawing on Curzon's knowledge of Klingon ways, including the maxim cited here, reminded him, "No Klingon warrior would leave a comrade behind while he goes off to battle."

Deep Space Nine: Blood Oath

Klingons do not faint.

vulchoHbe' tlhInganpu'.

Klingons do not get sick.

ropchoHbe' tlhInganpu'.

Klingons do not lie in bed.

QongDaqDaq Qotbe' tlhInganpu'.

Although these phrases are hyperbolic and known to be not literally true, there is a great deal of disgrace attached to being incapacitated, however briefly, and a general distrust of medicine. As other sayings have illustrated, Klingons value being in control, so having the need for medical intervention is a sign not only of physical weakness but of spiritual weakness. As the Klingon Kras put it when describing the Klingon attitude about ill health to the Capellans, "The sick should die. Only the strong should live."

As a member of Starfleet, Worf had voiced these and similar platitudes from time to time. He has an added reason to adhere to this virtue: A medical officer can override even a commanding officer's orders and is therefore always a potential threat to one's ability to maintain control.

As the only Klingon on the *Enterprise*, it is up to Worf to teach his shipmates Klingon ways.

The Next Generation: Up the Long Ladder
The Next Generation: Ethics
The Original Series: Friday's Child

Marc Okrand

Worf passes the rite marking the anniversary of his Age of Ascension.

To understand life, endure pain.

yIn DayajmeH 'oy' yISIQ.

Lieutenant Commander Data, an android who served as operations manager aboard the *Enterprise*, noted that "enduring physical suffering is considered a Klingon spiritual test," the idea embodied in this aphorism.

The Next Generation: The Icarus Factor

ROBBIE ROBINSON

Although half-human, Ambassador K'Ehleyr understands what it is to be Klingon.

Pleasure is nonessential.

'utbe' bel.

This Klingon truism is heard, in one form or another, again and again and probably dates back to ancient times, when warfare was carried out not in space vessels, but on fields where only the most indispensable supplies could be carried. Not only are considerations such as comfort, ease, and enjoyment not part of the Klingon way of thinking, to find them even desirable might be considered a sign of weakness. Thus, Worf explained to Riker, "I am not concerned with pleasure. . . . I am a warrior." The Klingon emissary K'Ehleyr, who was half-human and half-Klingon and therefore tended to view much of Klingon culture from a unique perspective, noted that "Klingons are not supposed to mind hardship."

On the other hand, it is assumed that non-Klingons do not share this sentiment. When showing Picard and Data their slablike beds on his ship, Klingon Captain K'Vada said, "You'll sleep Klingon style. We don't soften our bodies by putting down a pad." Though Klingon ships certainly could be designed to include various amenities, there is never any thought given to doing so. As Klingon Captain Koloth told Captain Kirk, "We do not equip our ships with . . . nonessentials."

The Next Generation: Shades of Gray
The Next Generation: The Emissary
The Next Generation: Unification
The Original Series: The Trouble With Tribbles

A warrior does not complain about physical discomfort.

loQ 'oy'DI' SuvwI' bepbe'.

The social stigma attached to incapacitation extends to perception: Whatever one's health, one does not want to be known as anything less than fully vigorous. The Federation Standard word "discomfort" somewhat distorts the meaning of the Klingon, which refers to a warrior "aching slightly."

The Next Generation: Clues

Klingons never bluff.

not toj tlhInganpu'.

Masked by its simplicity, this is actually a very clever Klingon epigram. If Klingons do indeed never resort to deception, the statement (more literally, "Klingons never deceive") expresses the truth. If, on the other hand, Klingons do mislead, then the statement is an example of that practice in action. Worf had made use of this phrase quite appropriately during games of poker.

The Next Generation: The Emissary

Adhere to virtue honorably.

batlh ghob yIpab.

This maxim, one of several about virtue itself, illustrates the importance of virtue in Klingon society. Not only should one be virtuous ("adhere to virtue"), that is, behave in a way Klingons consider morally righteous, one should take care to honor and respect those values. In other words, one should not merely endorse the values of the society, one should fully embrace their spirit and meaning. The Klingon verb in the expression, "**pab**," is here translated "adhere," but it is also used to mean "follow," in the sense of following rules, suggesting perhaps that, though not officially laws, virtues should be followed as if they were.

Virtue is the reward.

pop 'oH ghob'e'.

The Klingon word "**pop**" ("reward") could refer to compensation or a prize of some sort, but it also means "honor" in the sense of recognition for a particular achievement or set of achievements. This proverb does not mean "Virtue is honor." The use of the word "**pop**" suggests that virtue is the honor bestowed as a result of acting in a manner respectful of society's values, not simply advocating them.

One need not enjoy virtue.

ghob tIvnISbe'lu'.

Since, as noted earlier, Klingons find pleasure nonessential, it is not surprising to find virtue described as something that is not enjoyable. On the other hand, this aphorism does not say that virtue is never enjoyable, only that it is not necessarily so. The Klingon construction "**tIvnISbe'**" means "does not need to enjoy"; "**tIvbe'nIS**" would mean "needs to not enjoy," an utterly different concept. Leading a virtuous life may well be enjoyable, but if it is not, or if it is not always, it should still be done.

There is always a chance.

reH 'eb tu'lu'.

After Starfleet arranged for war exercises in which Commander Riker captained the eighty-year-old *Hathaway*, Riker lamented that his ship was no match for the *Enterprise*. Even if it was just a simulation, he felt there was no way he could win. Worf, believing that, as the Klingons say, "There is always a chance," suggested that what one lacks in physical power one makes up for with guile.

The common Klingon sendoff, "**Qapla'**," "success," is another overt signal of this warrior spirit: success is always possible.

The Next Generation: Peak Performance

The new security officer offers advice to his captain.

Capture all opportunities.

Hoch 'ebmey tIjon.

Worf passed this Klingon wisdom on to Picard when he said, "We may only have one opportunity; we should seize it." In Klingon, opportunities are captured, not taken; a missed opportunity is said to have escaped.

The Next Generation: The Neutral Zone

Worf's newly discovered brother brings him word of the charges of treason against their father.

Honor is more important than life.

batlh potlh law' yIn potlh puS.

Kurn, Worf's brother, said, "A Klingon's honor means more to him than his life." Worf passed the belief on to his son, Alexander: "A Klingon's honor is more important to him than his life. A Klingon would gladly face the most horrible punishment rather than bring shame or disgrace to his family name."

The degree to which this Klingon virtue is revered is perhaps best illustrated by an action of Lieutenant Commander Worf. The lieutenant commander was unwilling to join Gowron, leader of the High Council, in his invasion of Cardassia in part because to do so would have required him to renounce his oath of allegiance to Starfleet and the Federation. Gowron told Worf that this rejection carried serious consequences: Worf would be unwelcome in the Klingon Empire, his brother would be removed from the High Council, his family would lose its lands and titles. "You will be left with nothing," Gowron said. Worf encapsulated the true nature of being a Klingon with his reply, "Except my honor."

The Next Generation: Sins of the Father
The Next Generation: New Ground
Deep Space Nine: The Way of the Warrior

ROBBIE ROBINSON

Worf finds that the uniform of the Empire is not an easy fit.

One does not achieve honor while acting dishonorably.

batlhHa' vanglu'taHvIS quv chavbe'lu'.

Kurn, wanted to join the rebellion against Gowron, who was about to be installed as leader of the Klingon High Council. Gowron refused to overturn Worf's discommendation, the penalty of banishment and public disgrace accepted by the lieutenant commander after his unsuccessful challenge to the charge that his father was a traitor. Worf felt that Gowron was the only rightful leader of the Klingons and told his brother to support Gowron. "We cannot regain honor by acting dishonorably," he said. Later, Kurn's intervention helped to turn away an attack on Gowron by followers of the family of Duras. To reward them, Gowron, now the leader of the Council, restored their family honor.

The Next Generation: Redemption

When you insult a Klingon's honor, prepare for trouble.

tlhIngan quv DatIchDI' Seng yIghuH.

Klingon scientist Kurak was thinking of this aphorism when she informed Dr. Crusher, "Insulting the honor of a Klingon can be extremely dangerous."

The Next Generation: Suspicions

If you cannot fail, you cannot succeed.

bIlujlaHbe'chugh bIQaplaHbe'.

This maxim might also be translated as "If you cannot lose, you cannot win." Worf told Riker, "If there is nothing to lose—no sacrifice—there is nothing to gain."

The Next Generation: Peak Performance

If you cannot be shamed, you cannot be honored.

bItuHlaHbe'chugh bIquvlaHbe'.

Honor, it would appear, cannot exist in a vacuum. One cannot experience the feelings associated with honor unless one has the capacity to feel and understand the utter lack of it.

It is interesting to note how the Federation's perception of the Klingons has changed over the years. Initially, only the Klingons' warlike nature was noted. Klingons were viewed two-dimensionally and described as brutal and ruthless. Little else of their nature was known or, for the most part, cared about. Following the Khitomer peace conference, relations between the Federation and the Empire gradually improved. Fifty years later, Captain Rachel Garrett, in command of the *U.S.S. Enterprise* NCC-1701-C, would consider Klingons to be people, not objects of derision, and would render aid to a Klingon outpost on Narendra III, which was being attacked by Romulans. This action helped greatly in solidifying the Federation-Klingon alliance. Within the next twenty years, a Klingon, Worf, would join Starfleet and serve aboard a Federation ship, and a Starfleet officer, Picard, would actually participate in the process to choose a new Klingon leader. Recent events regarding the invasion of Cardassia notwithstanding, the Klingons are now seen to have a complex, multilayered culture, in which not only combativeness and aggressiveness are valued, but honor, loyalty, and virtue play key roles.

His own machinations lead K'mpec (Charles Cooper) to choose a human as the Arbiter of Succession.

The Klingon who kills without showing his face has no honor.

quv Hutlh HoHbogh tlhIngan 'ach qabDaj 'angbe'bogh.

This is an adage about Klingon behavior cited by K'mpec, leader of the Klingon High Council, when he revealed to Picard that he had been poisoned. Worf took it one step further, assuming that, since no Klingon would behave in such a dishonorable fashion, the assassination could not have been carried out by a Klingon. "A Klingon would not use poison," he stated. "The murder would have no honor."

The Next Generation: Reunion

ROBBIE ROBINSON

His is an old and honored house, with a deep affinity for the teachings of Kahless.

Only an enemy without honor refuses to show himself in battle.

'ang'eghQo' quv Hutlhbogh jagh neH ghobtaHvIS ghaH.

As is often the case, people assume that the values of their culture are shared by other cultures, whether or not this is the reality. Thus, as this variation of the preceding maxim suggests, it is considered dishonorable for anyone, not just a Klingon, to battle covertly. It is probably because of this belief that Klingons have never engaged in wide-scale guerrilla warfare.

The Next Generation: Evolution

ROBBIE ROBINSON

Counselor Troi (Marina Sirtis) tries to help Worf understand the human ways of dealing with death after a member of his away team was killed.

A leader must stand alone.

nIteb SuvnIS DevwI'.

Navigate your vessel alone.

nIteb DujlIj yIchIj.

Worf cited the first of these similar maxims to Counselor Troi when she suggested that he talk about his feelings. As with many Klingon sayings, it is framed in terms of confrontation. It literally means "A leader must fight alone." It refers to a basic tenet of Klingon society, self-sufficiency.

The Next Generation: The Bonding

Kurn takes up the duties of Worf's cha'DIch before the High Council.

May your enemies run with fear.

ghIj qet jaghmeyjaj.

As with common sayings in other languages, some Klingon proverbs, particularly those which have taken on ritualistic overtones, exhibit unusual grammatical forms. For instance, the Federation Standard, "If it ain't broke, don't fix it," exhibits nonstandard grammar, but it is still understood by all and is almost always heard in this form. Similarly, the commonly heard version of this Klingon expression, as uttered by Kurn and cited above, is grammatically aberrant. If the expression were rendered in everyday Klingon, it would be "**jaghmeylI' DaghIjjaj, qetjaj jaghmeylI'**" ("May you scare your enemies, may your enemies run").

The Next Generation: Sins of the Father

For one mission, there is one leader.

wa' Qu'vaD wa' DevwI' tu'lu'.

Though phrased in what could be considered militaristic terms ("**Qu'**," "mission," and "**DevwI'**," "leader"), this proverb is also often applied figuratively. If "mission" is interpreted to stand for the way one conducts one's life, the overall meaning is "one must guide oneself." It is yet another example of the Klingon virtue of self-sufficiency.

A Klingon does not postpone a matter of honor.

batlh qelDI' tlhIngan, lumbe'.

As several of these sayings make clear, nothing is more important to a Klingon than honor. When the Klingon officer Kulge questioned Gowron's leadership abilities, Gowron interrupted a strategy-planning session to engage him in a fight, eventually killing him, even though this delayed necessary planning for an ongoing war. To an outsider, Gowron's priorities might seem skewed, but to a Klingon, he acted properly. Even affairs of the Empire must take a back seat to protecting one's honor.

The Next Generation: Redemption

DANNY FELD

Koloth encounters a guard of the Albino and teaches him a proverb.

It is a good day to die.

Heghlu'meH QaQ jajvam.

This is an extremely common Klingon locution, often uttered when the odds seem to favor an opponent. It does not, however, represent a defeatist attitude. Quite the contrary, in a society in which warriors are so revered, to die in battle is a noble aspiration. Kang, of course, spoke ironically when, accepting the proposition that there was a chance to defeat an adversary, he altered this expression to "It is a good day to live."

The Next Generation: Sins of the Father
Deep Space Nine: Blood Oath

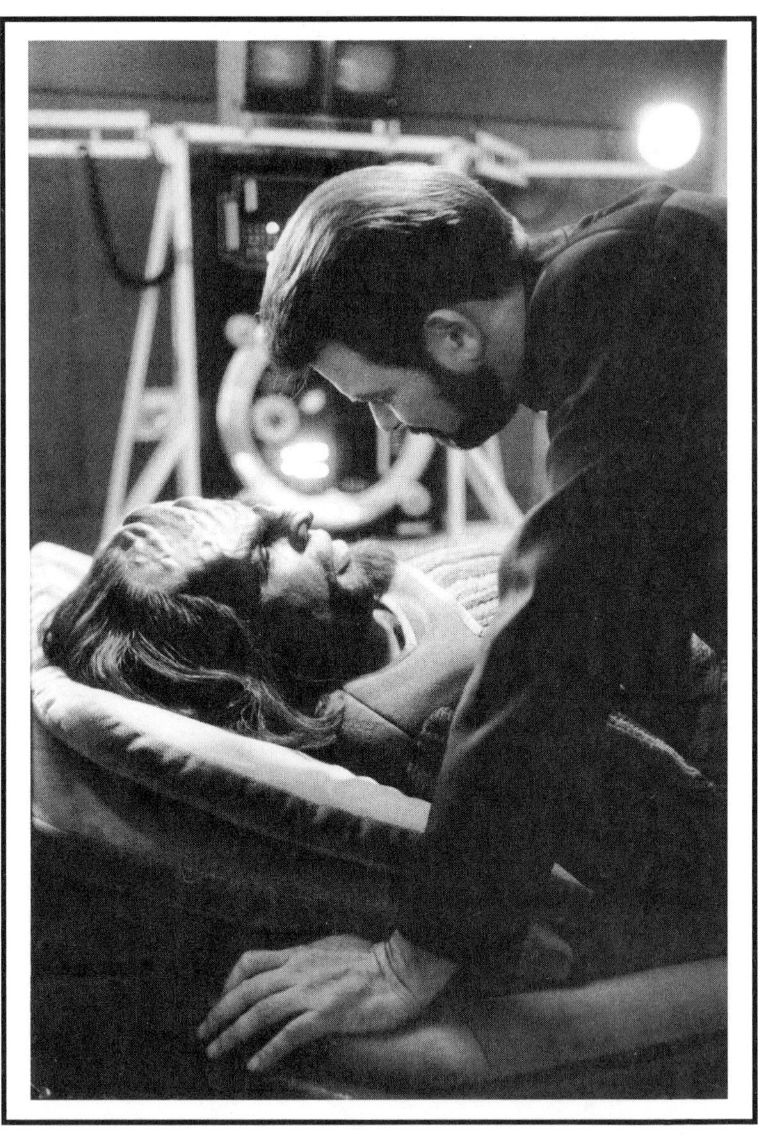

Commander Riker understands how Worf feels, but he will not aid in his friend's suicide.

May you die well.

batlh bIHeghjaj.

To die well—that is, honorably, in battle—is the desire of every Klingon. Captain Larg offered this proposition as a toast to Kurn when they were drinking in a Klingon tavern, celebrating their upcoming confrontation. Though enemies, they were, above all else, Klingons, and fortunate ones at that, for soon they would engage in fierce combat.

Any other sort of death, however, is a different matter. When, due to an accident, Worf was unable to walk, he felt his life was over. He believed that he would not be able to participate in future battles and therefore would not die in one. As a result, he chose to take his own life in a form of ritual suicide. Though he saw no alternative, he knew he would not "die well." As he told Riker, "I do not welcome death."

The Next Generation: Redemption
The Next Generation: Ethics

If you are afraid to die, you have already died.

bIHeghvIpchugh bIHeghpu'.

Worf was referring to death resulting from a battle when he told a noncorporeal criminal life-form which had possessed Data and had tried to goad the Klingon into attacking him, "I have no fear of death." One of the Klingons' most powerful motivations when engaging in battle is the possibility that they will die a glorious and honorable death in that confrontation. To feel otherwise, to fear an honorable death, is to resist a basic Klingon passion. Lacking this spark, this reason to go on, is equivalent, in the Klingon way of seeing things, to not living at all.

The Next Generation: Power Play

Death is an experience best shared.

Heghlu'DI' mobbe'lu'chugh QaQqu' Hegh wanI'.

One of the purposes of the Klingon Tea Ceremony, in which two friends share poisoned tea as a test of bravery, is to remind one of this truism. The ceremony, which is usually observed in periods of relative calm, between wars, probably came about as a way to reinforce and celebrate certain beliefs about warfare so central to Klingon culture. The ceremony symbolically acknowledges the dignity of death in battle, and it also pays tribute to warriors who battle alongside one another.

The Next Generation: Up the Long Ladder

To really succeed, you must enjoy eating poison.

bIQapqu'meH tar DaSop 'e' DatIvnIS.

This proverb suggests that the road to success is filled with peril, intrigue, risk, double-dealing, and other challenges to one's existence. To be truly successful, one must not only deal with such hazards, one must revel in doing so. Klingons have always considered it truly invigorating to face danger. As Commander Kruge said to Captain Kirk while the Genesis planet on which they were stranded was quickly falling apart, "Exhilarating, isn't it?"

Star Trek III: The Search for Spock

To die defending his ship is the hope of every Klingon.

DujDaj HubtaHuIS Hegh 'e' tul Hoch tlhIngan.

To die in the line of duty is the hope of every Klingon.

Qu'Daj ta'taHvIS Hegh 'e' tul Hoch tlhIngan.

To die while serving the Empire is the hope of every Klingon.

wo' toy'taHvIS Hegh 'e' tul Hoch tlhIngan.

Klingons are very concerned about their manner of death, so there are a number of relevant—and similar—sayings. Running through all of them is the idea that one's death should be honorable and purposeful. Clearly this applies to warriors, but since not everyone can be a warrior, Klingons also value other forms of duty and service to the Empire. Worf, then, reacted appropriately when, upon learning that someone had died in his sleep, remarked, "What a terrible way to go." This applies not only to Klingons, but to their friends. Thinking that Geordi La Forge had died, Worf told

ROBBIE ROBINSON

A force of the Klingon Empire invades space station Deep Space 9

Data, "For a Klingon, this is a joyful time. A friend has died in the line of duty."

The Next Generation: Power Play
The Next Generation: The Bonding
The Next Generation: The Royale
The Next Generation: The Next Phase

DANNY FELD

Strategy is honed before the fortress of the Albino is stormed.

A Klingon warrior is always prepared to fight.

reH Suvrup tlhIngan SuvwI'.

In Klingon it is not customary to say "to be prepared" without saying what one is prepared to do. There are, consequently, several versions of this proverb, the general meaning of which is "A Klingon warrior is always prepared." As called for by the situation, a specific activity is plugged in. Kang, for example, said, "A Klingon warrior is always prepared to die" ("**reH Heghrup tlhIngan SuvwI'**") It is even acceptable to use this proverb for less weighty matters, such as to eat and to drink. Not unexpectedly, using it to refer to an activity not prized by Klingons, such as to flee, to surrender, or to apologize, is particularly insulting.

Deep Space Nine: Blood Oath

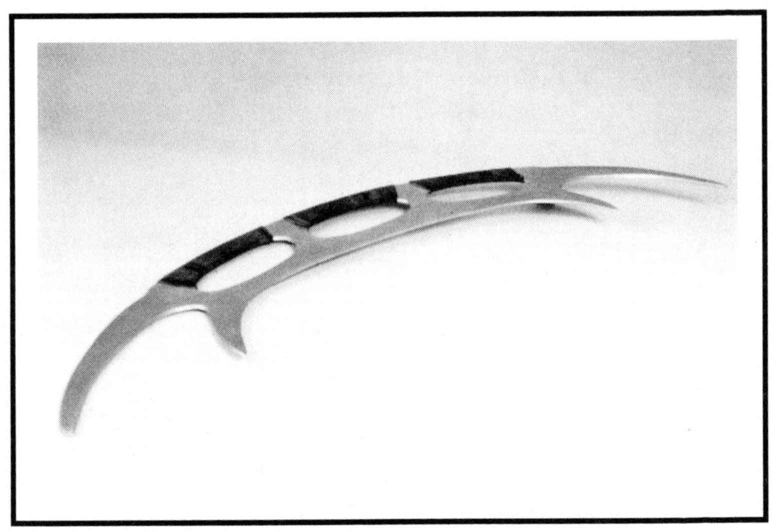

The honor blade of the House of Worf.

Never leave without your bat'telh.

bImejDI' reH betleHIIj yItlhap.

The bat'telh ("**betleH**"), sometimes called the "sword of honor," is probably the most Klingon of weapons. The original bat'leth was forged by Kahless the Unforgettable himself and, as a result, the weapon has rich cultural significance, not just sharp edges. This traditional admonition has a dual interpretation: As you venture out, always be prepared, and always maintain your identity as a Klingon.

No Klingon ever breaks his word.

not lay'Ha' tlhIngan.

Worf used this dictum when teaching his son, Alexander, about Klingon ways. He also taught that a Klingon's "word is his bond. Without it, he is nothing." Within the Klingon Empire, there are no written treaties. Apparently, because of this virtue of integrity, there is no need. This has caused conflicts from time to time in dealing with the Federation, which prefers documentation.

The Next Generation: Cost of Living
The Next Generation: New Ground

Focus on but one target.

wa' DoS neH yIbuS.

Though cast in warrior's terms, this dictum is really about priorities of any kind. It suggests that one should concentrate all one's attention on the task at hand and not try to do several things at once. Worf expresses the same conviction when referring to poker: "Talk or play, not both."

The Next Generation: The Emissary

ROBBIE ROBINSON

A Klingon actor plays the part of Molor (John Kenton Shull). It is Molor who is attributed with first saying "You salute the stars" to Kahless.

You salute the stars.

Hovmey Davan.

This is an unusual, but not unique, saying because it refers to a legend that must be known in order for the phrase to be understood. Outside the Empire, the details of this particular legend are quite sketchy, but the story seems to have something to do with a warrior who is about to be executed and asks for permission to go off alone, unguarded, in order to salute the stars a final time. Sometimes the warrior is said to have wanted to "say farewell" to the stars. Saying farewell, of course, is an artifact of translation. Under most circumstances, a Klingon would never literally say "farewell" or "good-bye" upon taking his leave; he would simply walk away. If, however, he wanted to show honor or respect, he may offer a salute, often verbalized as "**Qapla'**" ("success"). The request was granted, since, even in ancient times, it was known that a warrior keeps his word. Thus, "You salute the stars" means "I trust you" or "I know you will honor your word."

ROBBIE ROBINSON

The duty of maintaining tradition falls to the only Klingon to wear a Starfleet uniform.

A beard is a symbol of courage.

toDuj 'oS rol.

Though Klingons have a vast array of power weapons, the purest form of combat is hand-to-hand. Fighting in such close proximity to one another, a beard may be thought of by some as a disadvantage since one of the combatants may grab onto the beard of the other and draw him closer. To wear a beard, and long hair for that matter, shows that one is both brave and confident—willing to give the opponent the upper hand, and secure that one's own skills are superior.

The Next Generation: The Quality of Life

ROBBIE ROBINSON

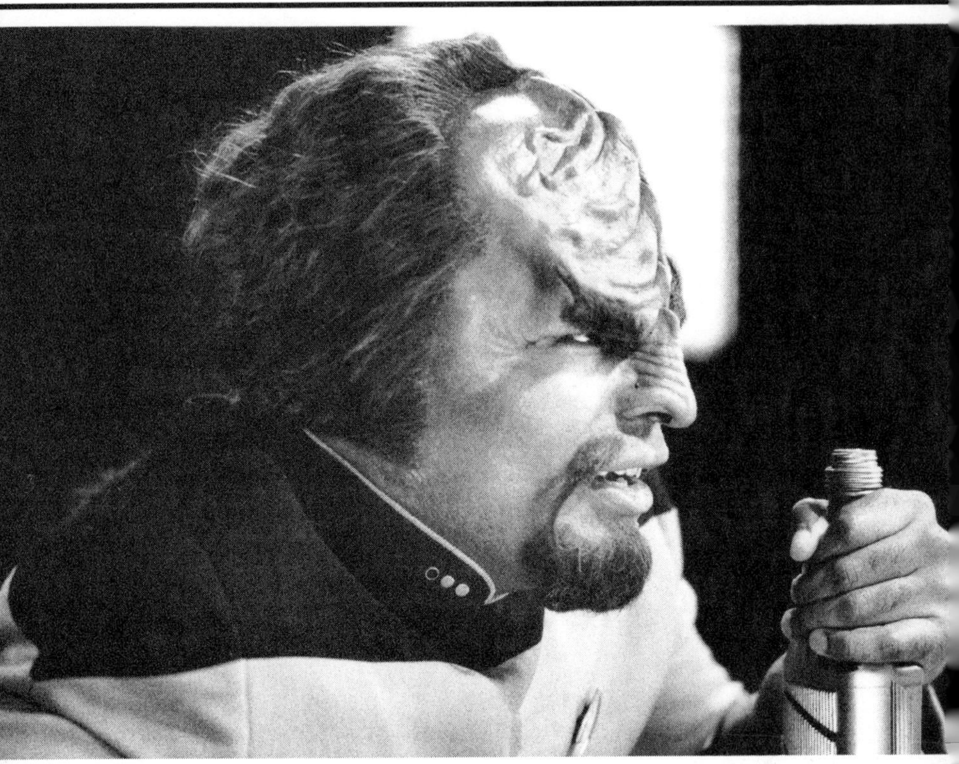

Not prune juice, this time.

Stop talking! Drink!

bIjatlh 'e' yImev. yItlhutlh!

Lieutenant Commander Worf has modified this old Klingon expression to a form more suitable for the *Enterprise:* "Less talk, more synthehol." Though he would prefer a true warrior's drink, while on a Federation starship he must make do with the available fare.

The Next Generation: Transfigurations

A warrior fights to the death.

wej Heghchugh vay', SuvtaH SuvwI'.

A somewhat more literal translation of this expression is "If someone has not yet died, a warrior keeps on fighting." That is, it does not matter who dies, but the fight is not over until one of the combatants is killed. As will be seen in a number of sayings cited later on, Klingons attach little if any value to prisoners. Only those lacking virtue would allow themselves to be taken prisoner in the first place. A true warrior and, by extrapolation, an opponent worthy of a true warrior would rather die.

The Next Generation: Birthright

Klingons do not surrender.

jeghbe' tlhInganpu'.

In order to stop the torturing of Ensign Chekov by the Klingons, James Kirk agreed to let Kang take over the *Enterprise*. Chekov protested, referring to the Klingons as animals, but Commander Kang thought the epithet was misplaced. "Animals. Your captain crawls like one," he said. "A Klingon would never have surrendered."

Because of this Klingon trait, Klingon emissary K'Ehleyr argued against disabling a Klingon ship whose crew was unaware of the peace treaty between the Federation and the Empire. If the ship were merely disabled, she said, the ship's captain would "destroy it himself." Worf concurred by simply quoting the maxim: "Klingons do not surrender."

In Klingon, the word for "surrender," "**jegh**," also can be translated as "give up," in the sense of abandoning a project. Thus, the saying also means that Klingons are persistent or even obstinate. As Worf put it, "Klingons do not give up easily."

The Original Series: Day of the Dove
The Next Generation: The Emissary
Deep Space Nine: The Way of the Warrior

Worf listens to the lies about his father spread by the House of Duras.

A Klingon does not run away from his battles.

may'meyDajvo' Haw'be' tlhIngan.

This maxim also appears in other guises, depending on what it is a Klingon does not run from. The general meaning of all of them is that Klingons do not flee; they do not abdicate their responsibilities or avoid the consequences of their actions. For example, when Worf decided to challenge the charge of treason leveled against his father, he knew that he would have to accept the penalty—death—if unsuccessful. A Klingon does not run from a judgment against him.

The Next Generation: Birthright

ROBBIE ROBINSON

With a cross-cultural exchange, the Yridian (James Cromwell) comes to a closer understanding of Klingon culture.

May you die before you are captured.

Dajonlu'pa' bIHeghjaj.

As noted earlier, Klingons are not fond of the notion of prisoners. After Admiral Kirk killed Klingon Commander Kruge and took over his bird-of-prey, Maltz, the sole surviving Klingon crew member of that ship, requested that he be killed rather than be taken prisoner. To Maltz's chagrin, Kirk refused to do so. Worf is also aware of the attitude. "A Klingon would rather die than be taken prisoner," he responded when the Yridian Jaglom Shrek suggested that Mogh, Worf's father, might have been captured and be still living.

The Next Generation: Birthright

GREG SCHWARTZ

Chancellor Azetbur (Rosanna DeSoto) finds that even her closest advisor cannot accept the tentative steps towards peace.

Better to die on our feet than live on our knees.

QamvIS Hegh qaq law' torvIS yIn qaq puS.

More literally, this is "Dying while standing is preferable to living while kneeling." The grammatical construction is a bit aberrant; one would expect "**QamtaHvIS**" ("while continuing to stand") and "**tortaHvIS**" ("while continuing to kneel"). In proverbs, however, grammatical shortcuts are not uncommon. Even the Federation Standard might be considered somewhat incomplete. One would expect "*It is* better to die on our feet than *to* live on our knees."

Klingon Chancellor Azetbur said she believed that the Empire was on the verge of becoming "obsolete." Because the destruction of the moon Praxis had devastated the main energy production facility for the Empire. She argued that the Klingons had no choice but to engage in peace talks with the Federation. Her military advisor, Brigadier Kerla, disagreed, citing this maxim to express his opinion.

Star Trek VI: The Undiscovered Country

Finding members of the Federation team on the Genesis planet provides Commander Kruge (Christopher Lloyd) with the answers he needs.

Cowards take hostages. Klingons do not.

vubpu' jon nuchpu'. jonbe' tlhInganpu'.

This adage, quoted by Worf to *Enterprise* security chief Tasha Yar, explicitly expresses the Klingon idea that taking a hostage is not a courageous act. Nevertheless, under certain circumstances, Klingons do take prisoners. When Commander Kang believed Kirk had destroyed his ship, he claimed the *Enterprise* and told Kirk and his crew, "You are now prisoners of the Klingon Empire against which you've committed a wanton act of war." He even threatened to "kill one hundred hostages at the first sign of treachery." This was a pragmatic move on Kang's part, of course, since he needed the cooperation—coerced or otherwise—of Kirk to gain control of the starship.

Similarly, Commander Kruge seemed to violate the norm when he and his men came across a group of Federation citizens—Lieutenant Saavik, David Marcus, and a young Spock—on the Genesis planet and seized them. His intention was to interrogate them and learn about the Genesis torpedo, not to hold them as hostages. Thus, when Kirk unexpectedly showed up, it was happenstance, not cowardice, that put Kruge in the position of being able to take advantage of the situation. He used the three as bargaining chips to negotiate with Kirk for what he really wanted. In Kruge's mind, he had not run afoul of the Klingon virtue.

The Next Generation: Heart of Glory
The Original Series: Day of the Dove
Star Trek III: The Search for Spock

ROBBIE ROBINSC

Captain Picard (Patrick Stewart) understands when Worf assures him that there were "no survivors."

No one survived Khitomer.

QI'tomerDaq Heghpu' Hoch.

This adage refers to an event and states its meaning by way of reference rather than directly. A Klingon outpost on the planet Khitomer was attacked by Romulans, who presumably killed everyone there except the young Worf and his nursemaid, Kahlest, who were rescued by Starfleet. When, from time to time, a rumor surfaced that there were other survivors, the rumor was always quashed. If there were survivors, the thinking went, they must have been captured, which would mean there are Klingons somewhere being held prisoner. This is intolerable, since both they and their families would be dishonored, and it is summarily dismissed as an impossibility. The phrase, then, is used to mean that an unacceptable situation is being rejected or denied outright. The literal translation of the Klingon is a little more blunt: "Everyone died at Khitomer."

The Next Generation: Birthright

ROBBIE ROBINSON

The story is told of how the first bat'telh was forged.

Even the best blade will rust and grow dull unless it is cared for.

'etlh QorghHa'lu'chugh ragh 'etlh nIvqu' 'ej jejHa'choH.

This proverb was uttered by the clone of Kahless. Since he knew it, it must have been known in the time of the original Kahless, making it one of the oldest of the Klingon proverbs. Though couched in militaristic terms, the expression is also interpreted figuratively to mean that one must take care of oneself, both physically and spiritually.

The Next Generation: Rightful Heir

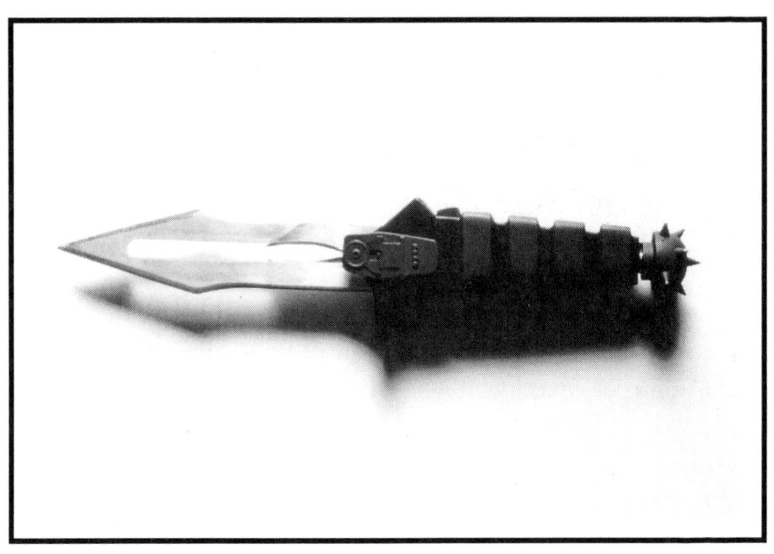

The traditional weapon of a Klingon assassin.

The used kut'luch is always shiny.

reH boch qutluch lo'lu'bogh.

The kut'luch ("**qutluch**") is a hand-held blade described as the ceremonial weapon of an assassin. Though cast in terms used referring to a murderer, a persona not unknown to Klingons, the proverb has a more general application. Only if one plies his trade or practices his art with some frequency will he remain at the peak of his skills.

The use of the kut'luch by assassins does not mean the weapon is used by no one else, nor does it mean that assassins never use other weapons. The way the weapon is used for ritual is utterly obscure, but the fact that the kut'luch has taken on a special status may explain why it has come to stand symbolically for assassination, perhaps in a manner that parallels the connection of "cloak and dagger" with intrigue and espionage on Earth.

Shooting space garbage is no test of a warrior's mettle.

vaj toDuj Daj ngeHbej DI vI'.

Captain Klaa, apparently for target practice, destroyed a defenseless Earth probe. He felt no sense of accomplishment and he complained to Vixis, his first officer, that what he had done was too easy and, therefore, unfulfilling. As Klaa knew, a warrior's skills must be proved not only continually, but meaningfully.

Star Trek V: The Final Frontier

Only fools have no fear.

not qoHpu''e' neH ghIjlu'.

Klingon warriors are reputed to be fearless in all situations, and they certainly behave that way. What this saying suggests is not that fear is not a factor, but rather that it is something to be understood and acted upon, not brushed aside. Worf tried to explain this to Wesley Crusher using this Klingon adage. On another occasion, Worf, suffering from severe sleep deprivation, said to Counselor Troi, "I am no longer a warrior. I am no longer strong. I feel fear." It was not the fear that caused him concern. It was his lack of ability to deal with it.

The Next Generation: Coming of Age
The Next Generation: Night Terrors

ROBBIE ROBINSON

Faced with Gowron's disbelief, Kahless recounts an ancient story.

The wind does not respect a fool.

qoH vuvbe' SuS.

This is actually the moral of a fable in the manner of Aesop. It advises one not to try that which is clearly impossible. According to the story, told by the clone of Kahless, a man once refused to go inside the city walls to protect himself from an impending storm. He said he wanted to "stand before the wind and make it respect me." The man was killed by the storm.

The Next Generation: Rightful Heir

ROBBIE ROBINSON

His position as leader of the High Council is not secure, and Gowron knows it.

Fear is power.

vay' DaghIjlaHchugh bIHoSghaj.

The meaning of this saying, of course, is that one who has the ability to instill fear can exert control over those who are afraid; there is more to power than physical force. Gowron quoted this Klingon truism when he told Picard that because the Duras sisters, Lursa and B'Etor, were feared, they had a strong and loyal following that posed a threat to Gowron's rule.

The Next Generation: Redemption

United against a common foe are wary allies — Klingon, human, and Vulcan.

Only a fool fights in a burning house.

meQtaHbogh qachDaq Suv qoH neH.

Even Klingons recognize that there are times not to fight, when battle is not productive. Kang quoted this proverb to the alien life form that caused his band of Klingons and Kirk's crew to engage in incessant bloodshed, informing the being that it had created circumstances that actually made combat inappropriate.

Significantly, the agreement by Kang and Kirk to stop fighting marked the first time that Klingons and humans cooperated of their own accord, foreshadowing the alliance between the Empire and the Federation years later. An earlier ban on hostilities between the two parties had been imposed from the outside by the powerful Organians.

The Original Series: Day of the Dove

Captain Kargan (Christopher Collins) explains the subtleties of Klingon strategy to his human first officer.

Only fools don't attack.

HIvbe' qoHpu' neH.

While Commander Riker was serving aboard the Klingon cruiser *Pagh* in an officer exchange program, a bacteria was discovered eating away the ship's hull. The Klingons blamed the *Enterprise* for this and resolved to destroy the Federation ship in retaliation. In the meantime, the *Enterprise* was searching for the *Pagh* in order to help rid the Klingon ship of the bacteria. Assuming, correctly, that the *Pagh* was cloaked in readiness for an attack, the *Enterprise* raised its shields, which the Klingons took as an act of aggression. Riker said that this was a precautionary measure, that the *Enterprise* would not fire first. Kargan, the *Pagh*'s captain, alluded to this proverb, saying, "Then they are fools, for we will."

It is most likely that this value applies only in situations of potential battle. A Klingon would find no honor in attacking an unarmed vessel without provocation.

The Next Generation: A Matter of Honor

ROBBIE ROBINSON

The drive of the Duras sisters, B'Etor (Gwynyth Walsh) and Lursa (Barbara Marsh), to control the High Council does not end with the death of their brother.

A fool's only achievement is death.

Hegh neH chav qoH.

When B'Etor told Picard that Duras was a fool, her sister Lursa remembered this expression. "He deserved to die," she said. Duras had sought to gain power in ways that were less than honorable. He used poison to kill Council Leader K'mpec, rather than challenging him face-to-face, and he altered Council records to hide his father's involvement in the Khitomer massacre. His sisters' held a low opinion of him, however, because he was ultimately unsuccessful.

The Next Generation: Redemption

ROBBIE ROBINSON

Highly skeptical of Kahless's "appearance," Gowron confronts the clerics from the monastery on Boreth.

Fools die young.

qanchoHpa' qoH, Hegh qoH.

As with all generalizations, exceptions are found to this maxim. Gowron once said to Koroth, "I see that not all fools die young," an insulting statement in light of Klingon belief.

The Next Generation: Rightful Heir

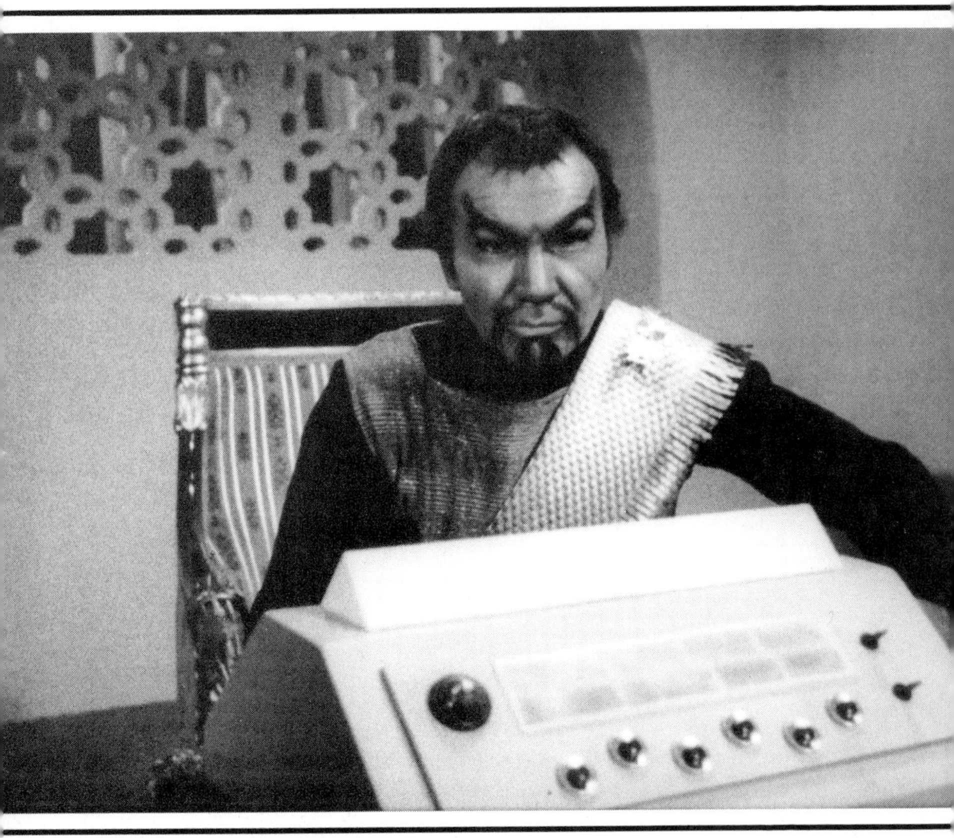

Secure in his power as military governor of Organia, Kor gloats over his captive.

Mercy or power.

pung ghap HoS.

Kor was thinking of this aphorism when he said to Kirk, "Ah, sentimentality, mercy—the emotions of peace. Your weakness, Captain Kirk." It is noteworthy that the conjunction in the Klingon phrase is "**ghap**" ("either/or"), not "**joq**" ("and/or"). This implies that one must choose between mercy and power; they are incompatible.

The Original Series: Errand of Mercy

Keep holding the hammer!

mupwI' yI'uchtaH!

As Data told Picard, the hammer is a symbol of power to Klingons. Thus, this exhortation is really saying to maintain power once it is achieved. The origin of the hammer's allegorical meaning is somewhat obscure, but it seems to have something to do with the way hammers were used to fashion weapons in ancient times. If one had a hammer, one could make one's own weapons and be self-sufficient. If one did not have a hammer, however, one was, at least to some degree, at the mercy of others.

The Next Generation: Birthright

Revenge is the best revenge.

bortaS nIvqu' 'oH bortaS'e'.

In Klingon society revenge is not merely a desirable response to an affront; it is, at least under some circumstances, a legal right called the Right of Vengeance (**bortaS DIb**). When Worf refused to kill Toral, the son of Duras, as revenge for the Duras family's role in dishonoring Worf's father, Kurn did not understand his brother's decision, since taking revenge is "the Klingon way." Kor, a highly honored Klingon captain, was equally incredulous: "A Klingon who denies himself the Right of Vengeance is no Klingon at all."

The Next Generation: Redemption
Deep Space Nine: The Sword of Kahless

Kor admires the virtues in one Organian, unaware that he is a Starfleet officer.

Always it is the brave ones who die.

reH Hegh yoHwI'pu''e'

Kor used this adage when speaking to the Organian Council of Elders. He amplified it a little, however, making it clear that he was referring to, in his word, "soldiers," though most Klingons would probably choose the term "warriors."

The Original Series: Errand of Mercy

ROBBIE ROBINSON

Worf tries to impart Klingon teachings to his son, Alexander (Jon Steuer).

Survival must be earned.

yInlu'taH 'e' bajnISlu'.

Victory must be earned.

yay chavlu' 'e' bajnISlu'.

These and similar maxims teach that Klingons believe one must work to attain what is wanted or needed. Kor's thoughts about survival are most basic, referring to life itself. Worf used a form of this expression when imparting Klingon values to Alexander. "You must earn victory," he told him, meaning earning it in an honorable fashion.

The Original Series: Errand of Mercy
The Next Generation: Reunion

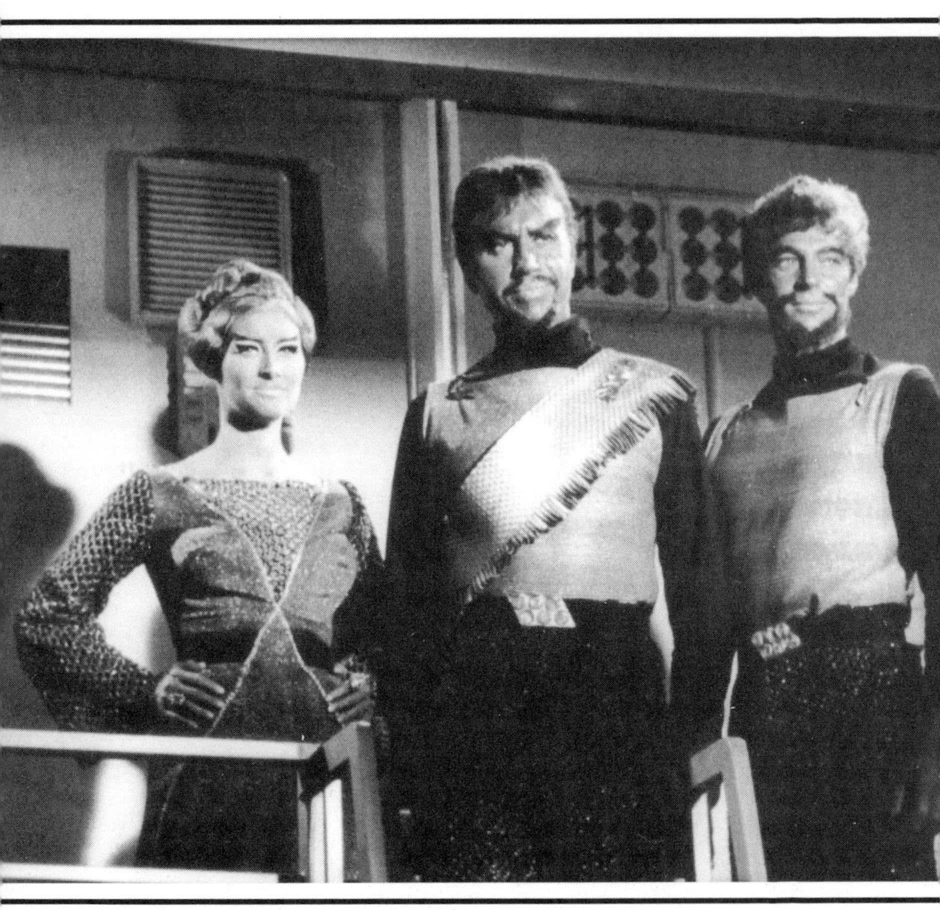

Imprisoned and outnumbered, the members of Kang's command take heed that not even a single Klingon can be discounted.

Four thousand throats may be cut in one night by a running man.

qaStaHvIS wa' ram loS SaD Hugh SIjlaH qetbogh loD.

Though he and his crew were prisoners of Captain Kirk, Klingon Commander Kang still planned to seize control of the *Enterprise*. Mara, his wife and science officer, felt they were at a numerical disadvantage. "We are forty against four hundred," she said. Klingons, however, are used to overcoming odds, just as they are used to overcoming the limited resources of their homeworld. One of Kang's crew reminded Mara of this by quoting this Klingon proverb, which addresses not only accomplishing what one sets out to do, despite the obstacles, but also the virtue of simply taking action.

The Original Series: Day of the Dove

ROBBIE ROBINSON

The widow of Kozak (Mary Kay Adams) seeks the "brave warrior" (Armin Shimerman) who "honorably" killed her husband.

An honorable death requires no vengeance.

batlh Heghlu'chugh noDnISbe' vay'.

After the Klingon Kozak died in Quark's bar on space station Deep Space 9, a Klingon claiming to be Kozak's brother came to ask Quark to explain the circumstances of Kozak's death. The Klingon told Quark that an accidental death is not honorable and that the dishonor, passed on to other members of Kozak's family, would require revenge. On the other hand, a death resulting from a battle is honorable and, as the adage states, "requires no vengeance." Though Kozak actually died when he fell on his own knife, to save himself Quark lies and says he killed Kozak in "a brave and valiant battle." In fact, the Klingon, D'Ghor, was not Kozak's brother at all but a member of a rival house. Their family stood to gain control over Kozak's property as long as there were no unusual circumstances surrounding Kozak's death, such as its being accidental. Citing this Klingon dictum helped D'Ghor persuade Quark to give the explanation most beneficial to D'Ghor.

Deep Space Nine: The House of Quark

GREG SCHWARTZ

Aboard a Starfleet ship, General Chang (Christopher Plummer) finds solace in "Klingon" literature.

Tickle us, do we not laugh? Prick us, do we not bleed? Wrong us, shall we not seek revenge?

cheqotlhchugh maHaghbe''a'? cheDuQchugh mareghbe''a'? cheQIHchugh manoDbe''a'?

These traditional lines, somewhat expanded, were used by Shakespeare, who, some Klingons claim, wrote plays in their language. General Chang was quite fond of quoting the Bard.

Star Trek VI: The Undiscovered Country

BRUCE BIRMELIN

Khan Noonien Singh (Ricardo Montalban) relates this proverb to his "old friend" Admiral James Kirk.

Revenge is a dish which is best served cold.

bortaS bIr jablu'DI' reH QaQqu' nay'.

This old Klingon proverb is known beyond the Empire. For example, it was cited by Khan Noonien Singh, a genetically engineered human who ruled much of the Earth tyrannically in the late twentieth century. He had escaped in a sleeper ship and remained in suspended animation until awakened in the twenty-third century when he was rescued by the *U.S.S. Enterprise* NCC-1701. Khan must have learned of this expression when he was studying material in Federation data banks. Though, as far as is known, Khan never had any direct contact with Klingons, he shared at least one attitude with them: a need for revenge when wronged. Khan died while trying to take revenge on James T. Kirk, whom he felt had abandoned him on what became an uninhabitable planet.

Star Trek II: The Wrath of Khan

Raised among humans, the son of Mogh still finds them a puzzle.

If winning is not important, then why keep score?

potlhbe'chugh yay qatlh pe''eghlu'?

This adage is phrased as a rhetorical question, and Worf used it that way after Riker told him that the main reason to play a game of parrises squares is to have fun. It is possible that this expression is relatively new, one that arose after contact with humans who would be heard saying such things as, "Winning isn't everything" or "It's not whether you win or lose, it's how you play the game." From the Klingon point of view, such a position is, at the very least, odd. Since humans persist in this way of looking at things, however, Worf may have decided to simply opt out of situations where this attitude presents itself. Thus, when invited by Dr. Julian Bashir and Chief Miles O'Brien to join them in a game of darts, the Klingon replied, "I do not play games." After O'Brien described the activity as target practice, however, the lieutenant commander agreed to participate.

The Klingon way to say "keep score" is "**pe''egh,**" literally, "cut oneself." It comes from an old Klingon habit of keeping track of accomplishments by making small cuts on one's skin, usually on the face, as a tally. Perhaps coincidentally, Klingons' faces are often similarly scratched following romantic encounters.

The Next Generation: 11001001
Deep Space Nine: The Way of the Warrior

The execution of but one warrior brings shame to all.

wa' SuvwI' muHlu'DI', tuHchoH Hoch SuvwI'pu'.

Worf recognized that Klingon renegades Korris and Konmel must be punished, but because they were Klingons, he felt they should be allowed to "meet death on their feet with a weapon in their hands, not tied and helpless." To be executed as a prisoner is to die dishonorably, and this dishonor reflects on Klingons in general. K'nera, who had come to take the rebels back to the Klingon Homeworld, agreed. "When one of us dies that way," he said, alluding to the well-known Klingon adage, "it diminishes us all." To the Klingon way of thinking, being held captive is not only a disgrace, the very notion of a Klingon prisoner is an oxymoron.

The Next Generation: Heart of Glory

He doesn't eat gagh!

qagh Sopbe'!

Everyone loves gagh, so if one is not eating it, something must be wrong. This expression is used to mean that there is something wrong with someone or that someone is acting suspiciously. It is also a way to refer to somebody as a coward.

For Klingons, among whom cursing is a highly developed art form, this is a rather mild dismissive remark, not a strong insult. As this expression demonstrates, even though Klingon culture is known for its directness, it is also capable of expressing ideas subtly.

Worf knows his is the heart of a warrior.

If a warrior ignores duty, acts dishonorably, or is disloyal, he is nothing.

Qu' buSHa'chugh SuvwI', batlhHa' vangchugh, qoj matlhHa'chugh, pagh ghaH SuvwI''e'.

Klingon Commander Korris, who strongly opposed the Federation-Klingon alliance, tried to convince Worf to give up Starfleet and join with him to live the life of a "true" Klingon. Worf, however, thinking about the several virtues embodied in this adage, replied, "In all you say, where are the words 'duty,' 'honor,' 'loyalty,' without which a warrior is nothing?"

The Next Generation: Heart of Glory

A true delicacy that cannot be properly replicated.

Gagh is always best when served live.

yIntaHbogh qagh jablu'DI' reH nIvqu' qagh.

When Captain Klag said this to William Riker, he was speaking literally, actually talking about the Klingon delicacy gagh, or serpent worms. The same expression, however, is often used figuratively to mean that a fight is always better when there is a worthy adversary, or that one should always want to face real challenges.

The Next Generation: A Matter of Honor

Admire the person with dirt under his fingernails.

butlh ghajbogh nuv'e' yIHo'.

The Klingon word "**butlh**" ("dirt under fingernails") can be taken literally, but in this expression it means something like "effrontery, impudence, brazenness." The origin of this usage of the term is obscure, but it may be connected to the notion that one not having "**butlh**" is leading a soft, comfortable, not very Klingonlike life. To say to someone "**butlh DaHutlh**" ("You lack dirt under your fingernails") is highly insulting. It means that the person is lacking in a certain kind of Klingon spirit. In Federation Standard, an approximate equivalent is gall. Indeed, Worf said to Kevin Uxbridge, "Your attempt to hold the away team at bay with a nonfunctioning weapon was an act of unmitigated gall . . . I admire gall." Had Worf said that Uxbridge's action was "an act of unmitigated dirt under the fingernails," he would have been misunderstood, at the very least. The Klingon way to say, "you lack gall" is "**HuH DaHutlh.**" This is literally "You lack bile," and a Klingon would probably only understand it biologically.

The Next Generation: The Survivors

Motives are insignificant.

ram meqmey.

Kell, a Klingon working as a Romulan operative, tried to appeal to Worf's Klingon nature when he praised Worf for killing Duras. Worf protested that he did so for personal, not political, reasons. Kell took his cue from this Klingon adage. "Who cares for motives?" he said. "You acted that day as a true Klingon."

The Next Generation: The Mind's Eye

Voices are raised as a warrior's spirit travels to Sto-Vo-Kor.

When a warrior dies, his spirit escapes.

HeghDI' SuvwI' nargh SuvwI' qa'.

When a Klingon dies, it is thought that his spirit leaves his body and goes to join the spirits of other dead Klingons. This is marked in the Klingon Death Ritual when the surviving comrades howl—a warning to the dead that a warrior's spirit is on its way. The body, once the spirit has left it, is considered a worthless shell and is discarded unceremoniously. Exactly what Klingons think the spirit is doing when it leaves the body is a little unclear. The verb "**nargh,**" found in the saying cited above, means "escape," but the same word, or a phonetically identical one, means "appear." Thus, perhaps the Klingons are saying that when a warrior dies, his spirit appears, whereas prior to death it was hidden or disguised by the body. Another interpretation is that the spirit was held prisoner by the body. Worf told Jeremy, whose mother had been killed, "In my tradition, we do not grieve the loss of the body. We celebrate the releasing of the spirit."

The Next Generation: The Bonding

ROBBIE ROBINSON

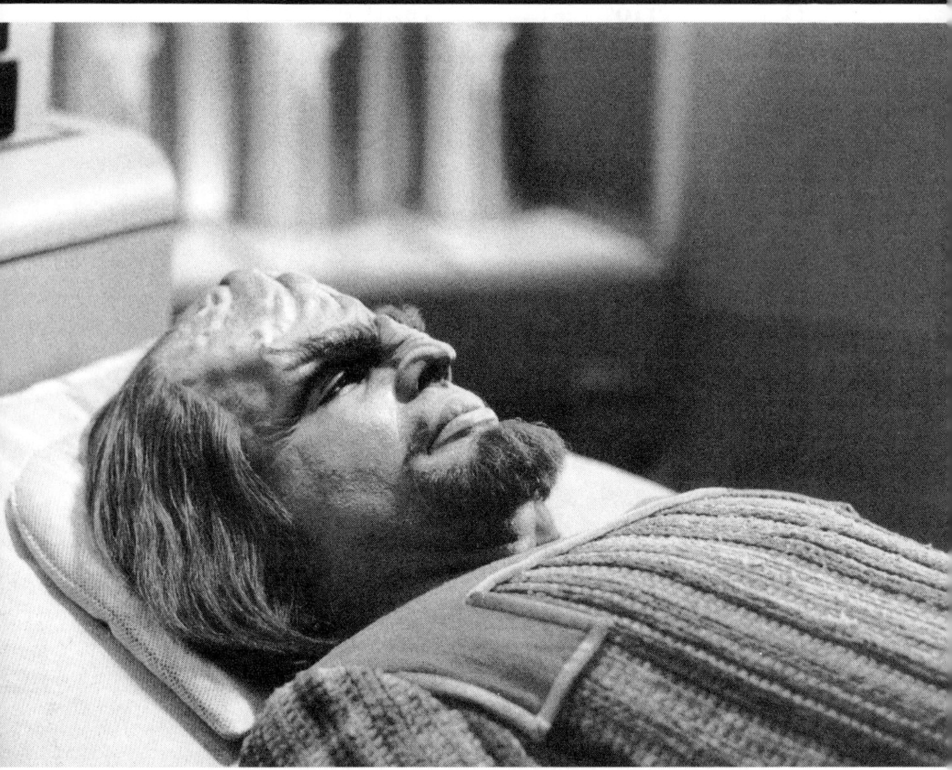

Determined to keep fighting, Worf makes a momentous and dangerous choice.

If the warrior's spirit has not escaped, the battle is still going on.

narghbe'chugh SuvwI' qa' taH may'.

This saying, which also contains the word **nargh** discussed on page 145, is used to caution the listener not to draw conclusions too soon. Its import resembles several twentieth-century Earth expressions beginning "It's not over until . . . "

After being paralyzed from the waist down as the result of an accident, Worf at first felt his life had ended and decided to commit ritual suicide ("**Heghbat**"). Later, he had a change of heart. Though this may have been because, as William Riker suggested, Worf did not want his son, Alexander, to participate in his father's death as would be required by the ritual, it may also have been because Worf remembered the teachings of this proverb. The warrior spirit was still within him; he would continue the battle and try a new form of therapy.

Curse well!

pe'vIl mu'qaDmey tIbach.

Cursing, or swearing, is considered a fine art among Klingons. One who curses well is the recipient of a great deal of respect; one who does not curse well may not be worthy enough to be called Klingon. Thus it was a compliment when Klingon Governor Vagh said, "You swear well, Picard. You must have Klingon blood in your veins." The commonly heard sendoff "Curse well!"—roughly comparable in usage to the Federation Standard "Good luck!"—literally means, "Shoot curses forcefully!" Curses are considered a weapon of a sort which must be propelled to their targets.

The Next Generation: The Mind's Eye

Conquer what you desire.

vay' DaneHbogh yIchargh.

The Klingon habit of "taking what we need," as Mara, Commander Kang's wife, put it, is a very basic element of the Klingon approach to life. Though she was speaking of food, land, and the like, the attitude is more pervasive. Worf referred to it when speaking of male-female relationships, telling Data, "Klingons do not pursue relationships. They conquer that which they desire."

Quark, the Ferengi barkeep on space station Deep Space 9, has had personal experience with the practical application of this Klingon attitude. Because he killed the Klingon Kozak, even though accidentally, Klingon custom allowed him to assume Kozak's position as leader of a family (or house) and to take Kozak's widow, Grilka. To maintain her position, and, since there was no male heir, to prevent her holdings from falling into others' hands, Grilka followed the advice of this Klingon adage: She conquered Quark. In a ceremony almost totally lacking in pomp, each made a short vow, (Quark's made under duress.) Grilka kissed him, and they were married.

The Original Series: Day of the Dove
The Next Generation: In Theory
Deep Space Nine: The House of Quark

Gowron offers Worf no support to overcome his discommendation.

You have chosen your weapon, so fight!

nuHIIj DawIvpu', vaj yISuv!

This phrase is often used in a figurative sense to mean that one must accept and deal with the consequences of one's choices. Gowron expressed the thought more literally: "Now you must live with your decision like a Klingon."

The Next Generation: Redemption

Seeing Worf puzzled by the revelry in a Klingon bar, Kurn reminds his brother of this warrior's cry.

Celebrate! Tomorrow we may die!

yIlop! wa'leS chaq maHegh!

Kurn reminded Worf that partaking in festivities, not elaborate planning, is the Klingon way the night before a battle: "You and I will fight battles others can only dream of. Our time for glory is here. This is not the time to worry about stabilizers. It is a time to celebrate, for tomorrow we may die." This ancient Klingon saying is unrelated to a similar expression heard on Earth, "Eat, drink, and be merry, for tomorrow we may die." The Klingon locution speaks of celebrating one's own impending, presumably honorable and glorious, death. The Terran version has come to mean "Enjoy yourself now; it may be your last chance."

The Next Generation: Redemption

Worf shoulders the burden of the accusations against his father.

The family of a Klingon warrior is responsible for his actions, and he is responsible for theirs.

vangDI' tlhIngan SuvwI' ngoy' qorDu'Daj; vangDI' qorDu'Daj ngoy' tlhIngan SuvwI'.

The dishonor of the father dishonors his sons and their sons for three generations.

qaStaHvIS wej puq poHmey vav puqloDpu' puqloDpu'chaj je quvHa'moH vav quvHa'ghach.

The bonds within a family, or house, are extremely strong in Klingon culture, as illustrated by these two maxims. Though the second is phrased in terms of male family members only, and a time frame of three generations is mentioned, this represents, so to speak, only the spirit of the law. In fact, when an individual is dishonored, the next several generations of his entire family are similarly dishonored, the period of time apparently depending on the circumstances of the initial offense or misfortune. When dishonored, members of the family may forfeit property as well as any position in the government. The greatest loss is the ability to walk proudly among other Klingons.

The Next Generation: Sins of the Father
The Next Generation: Birthright

ROBBIE ROBINSON

Toq (Sterling Macer, Jr.) reminds his elders of what it is to be truly Klingon.

Remember the scent.

vay' DalarghDI' yIqaw.

After de-evolving to a lizardlike state because a synthetic T-cell had invaded the DNA of the *Enterprise* crew, Worf pursued Deanna Troi. Captain Picard and Lieutenant Commander Data decided to reproduce Troi's pheromones and draw Worf away from her by spreading them around the ship. This would work, Picard reasoned, because of a notable fact about Klingons' genetic makeup. "Klingons have a highly developed sense of smell," he pointed out.

It is not surprising, then, that the sense of smell should have worked its way into the Klingon body of wise sayings. In teaching Toq, a young Klingon, about hunting, Worf used the phrase cited here literally, but it is often used figuratively, meaning something like "Learn from your experiences."

The Next Generation: Genesis
The Next Generation: Birthright

K'Ehleyr will not accept Worf's distance.

Love is always smelled.

reH bang larghlu'.

This phrase might be more literally translated as "A loved one is always smelled," in other words. One's strong feelings for someone are first aroused by the sense of smell. Speaking to Geordi La Forge about courting behavior, Worf put it a little more eloquently: "Words come later. It is the scent that first speaks of love."

The Next Generation: Transfigurations

A proud warrior finds it impossible that one of his own can wear the uniform of Starfleet and still be a Klingon warrior.

The hunter does not lie down with the prey.

QotDI' gheD tlhejbe' wamwI'.

The Klingon renegade Korris asked Worf, "What is it like for the hunter to lie down with the prey? Have they tamed you, or have you always been docile?" By likening a warrior to his prey and by suggesting that Worf had ignored the teaching of this proverb, Korris insulted Worf, probably more to make Worf angry than to offend him.

The Next Generation: Heart of Glory

ROBBIE ROBINSON

Awakened to what it is to be Klingon, Toq embraces the ancient warrior ways.

Do not kill an animal unless you intend to eat it.

Ha'DIbaH DaSop 'e' DaHechbe'chugh yIHoHQo'.

This admonishment against nonutilitarian killing was taught to the young Toq by Worf. It probably originated because the Klingon Empire has limited resources, none of which can be wasted. As Mara, Commander Kang's wife, explained, "There are poor planets in the Klingon system."

The Next Generation: Birthright
The Original Series: Day of the Dove

Presented with the opportunity to kill a Starfleet captain,
Kang refuses to be manipulated.

Klingons kill for their own purposes.

tlhIngan ngoQmey chavmeH
HoH tlhInganpu'.

Kirk convinced Commander Kang that an alien life force was causing the Klingons and the *Enterprise* crew to engage in ceaseless hostilities and that Kang was serving the whim of this alien being. Throwing down his weapon, Kang refused to go on fighting, citing a proverb that expresses the Klingon aversion to being dominated by others. More important even than following the instinct to be a warrior is the ability to maintain control over one's own actions.

The Original Series: Day of the Dove

The "placid sheep" of the Council and their smiles disgust Kor, who prefers the nonsmiling "Organian" beside him.

Don't trust those who frequently smile.

pIj monchugh vay' yIvoqQo'.

Kor harked back to this expression when he said, referring to the Organian Council of Elders, "I don't trust men who smile too much." To a Klingon, a smile signals not only contentment, satisfaction, and good humor, but also complacency, the feeling that all is well. This would imply there is no reason to do anything, no need to take action. For Klingons, who always feel the need to act, someone who seems to lack this need is either hiding something or is simply bizarre. In either case, such a person is likely to behave in an unreliable fashion.

The Original Series: Errand of Mercy

DANNY FELD

Koloth will let nothing come between him and his vengeance on the Albino.

A sharp knife is nothing without a sharp eye.

leghlaHchu'be'chugh mIn lo'laHbe' taj jej.

Three aging Klingon captains—Koloth, Kor, and Kang—got together on space station Deep Space 9 in order to plan the killing of an Albino marauder who had murdered the firstborn child of each, some eighty years earlier. While Kor thought his glories lay in the past, Koloth spent his time practicing and training in an effort to retain his skills. He quoted this Klingon adage to Kor as explanation for his actions.

The saying can be used more generally to mean that although good tools are important, it is the proficient user who actually accomplishes the job.

Deep Space Nine: Blood Oath

Your father is a part of you always.

reH DuSIgh vavlI'.

Worf explained to Data that learning about your father "tells you about yourself." Among Klingons, a son is known by the deeds of his father. The importance of one's father is demonstrated in the Klingon practice of using one's father's name in identifying oneself. Worf, for example, would say, "I am Worf, son of Mogh." Under some circumstances, one might even refer to him simply as "Son of Mogh" and not say "Worf" at all.

The Next Generation: Birthright

Pay no heed to glob flies.

ghIlab ghewmey tIbuSQo'.

A glob fly is a tiny Klingon insect that makes a loud buzzing sound but has no stinger. The proverb means "Don't pay attention to insignificant things."

GENE TRINDEL

A strange phenomenon reunites Worf with his childhood pet.

If you sleep with targs, you'll wake up with glob flies.

bIQongtaHvIS nItlhejchugh targhmey bIvemDI' nItlhej ghIlab ghewmey.

The targ, a furry Klingon animal that more or less resembles a Terran pig, is often kept as a pet. Indeed, Lieutenant Commander Worf had one when he was young. It is also a source of food, and heart of targ is a traditional Klingon dish. The tiny Klingon glob flies typically swarm about targs, undoubtedly making them that much more appealing. Pets, however, are for amusement; they are not associated with serious endeavors.

For a Klingon, sleeping is not only a time for revitalization of the body, it is also a time for spiritual or psychological renewal, with dreams playing an important role. Thus, the idea of sleeping with targs—or, as a more literal translation of the proverb might put it, being accompanied by targs while sleeping—suggests an association with trivial rather than weighty matters. The result is waking up with, perhaps being taken over by, glob flies, or insignificant thoughts. The message, then, is to maintain focus on that which is meaningful.

If the *qIvon* is cold, the blood is hot.

bIrchugh qIvon tuj 'Iw.

It is not clear what a **qIvon** is, aside from the fact that it is a Klingon body part, so the real meaning of the saying is a little obscure. It probably means something like "Even though some parts of the body may be cold, a Klingon's blood is hot"—that is, he is ready for battle.

No pain, no gain.

'oy'be'lu'chugh Qapbe'lu'.

This expression was apparently borrowed from an old expression used by some members of the Federation. Though proud of their uniqueness in the galaxy, Klingons willingly adopt—or, in true Klingon spirit, take—ideas from the outside if those ideas fit in with and support Klingon values.

ROBBIE ROBINSO

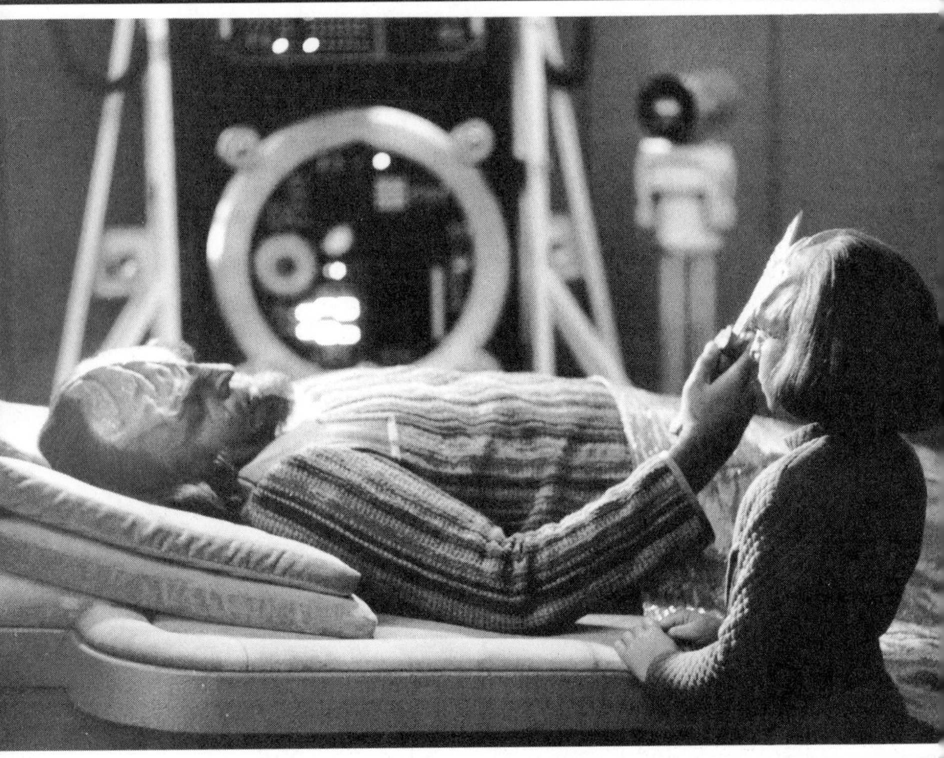

Trapped by his own traditions, Worf must ask Alexander (Brian Bonsall) to help with his suicide.

The son of a Klingon is a man the day he can first hold a blade.

wa' jaj 'etlh 'uchchoHlaH tlhIngan puqloD; jajvetlh loD nen moj.

This proverb, which Riker quoted to Worf, albeit in Federation standard, illustrates the importance of the blade—in some renditions of this proverb, a knife. It is a symbol of maturity as well as of self-reliance. Paralyzed from the waist down after an accident and feeling unable to continue as a warrior, Worf decided to commit suicide in the traditional Klingon manner, the **Heghbat**. He asked Riker to help him and hand him the knife, but Riker pointed out that, following tradition, that role belonged to Worf's son, Alexander. After Worf objected that Alexander was only a child, Riker argued that Alexander was old enough since, as the proverb says, he could hold a blade. Worf decided he did not want to put Alexander in the position of helping his father die, and chose the risky, but ultimately successful, genetronic replication therapy instead.

The Next Generation: Ethics

ROBBIE ROBINSON

The warrior spirit courses through him, and Gowron cannot bear to hear the platitudes of the Federation.

The victor is always right.

reH lugh charghwI'.

In war, there is nothing more honorable than victory.

noH ghoblu'DI' yay quv law' Hoch quv puS.

History is written by the victors.

qun qon charghwI'pu''e'.

All these sayings seem to contradict somewhat the Klingon belief that nothing is more important than honor itself. They make clear an ongoing struggle within Klingons between their craving for the glories of battle on the one hand and their veneration of honor on the other. They also show that Klingon and human characteristics are not totally at odds. For example, the first proverb echoes the old Earth saying "Might makes right." The third Klingon maxim, used by Gowron, says that victors (actually, "conquerors") "record" ("**qon**") history. It does not matter whether this recording is visual, digital, scratches in stone, or marks on paper.

Deep Space Nine: The Way of the Warrior

ROBBIE ROBINSON

The owner of the bar on Deep Space 9 finds his new regular . . . different.

To find ale, go into a bar.

HIq DaSammeH tach yI'el.

This is a commentary on not overlooking the obvious.

A ship cloaks in order to attack.

HIvmeH Duj So'lu'.

This phrase is used both literally and figuratively. General Koord said, "If my people are cloaked, then they intend to strike," paraphrasing the literal meaning of the expression. Figuratively, it can also refer to any situation where the observable facts lead to an obvious conclusion.

Because of the great amount of power required to remain cloaked, Klingon ships must decloak before actually firing any weapons. Thus, even though they may approach an enemy undetected, they strike secure in the knowledge that the adversary knows the identity of the attacker. This upholds the Klingon virtue, cited earlier, that the only honorable way to do battle is to show one's face. Klingon technology has long been advanced enough to create a cloaking device that does not have to be deactivated before firing, but Klingon morality discourages pursuing this option. The one time a ship was equipped with such a device, a conspiracy of Klingons and others, acting most dishonorably, used it to assassinate Klingon Chancellor Gorkon.

Star Trek V: The Final Frontier

In order to succeed, we attack.

maQapmeH maHIv.

This is an idea drilled into every Klingon's head. K'Ehleyr was aware of this when she predicted the actions of a Klingon ship: "They're Klingons! They'll attack!"

The Next Generation: The Emissary

Everyone encounters tribbles occasionally.

rut yIHmey ghom Hoch.

As is well known, Klingons find tribbles intolerable—and, apparently, vice versa. The expression, therefore, means that, from time to time, everyone has to deal with intolerable situations.

If you want to eat pipius claw, you'll have to break a few pipiuses.

pIpyuS pach DaSop DaneHchugh pIpyuS puS DaghornIS.

Pipius claw is a traditional Klingon dish. As with Klingon food in general, it is not cooked, but neither is a live or just-killed pipius simply thrown in front of the diner. The details of preparing pipius claw are not well understood, as Klingon chefs are notoriously protective of their recipes. It is believed that the pipius is torn apart and the various pieces are soaked in (or perhaps basted with) some kind of fluid of animal origin that adds flavor and chemically alters the texture of the pipius.

This proverb, however, is really not about food. It supports the Klingon virtues of conquering that which is desired and taking of action—breaking a few pipiuses. Indeed, on occasion, a modified version of the second part of this expression is used as a command to tell someone, often a child, to get started on or to devote more effort to a project: "**pIpyuS yIghor!**" ("Break a pipius!")

Trust, but locate the doors.

yIvoq 'ach lojmItmey yISam.

Trust, but verify.

yIvoq 'ach yI'ol.

These two adages offer the same advice: Even with those who appear to be honorable, ethical, and deserving of trust, one must always be careful. In the first expression, the Klingon word for "door," "**lojmIt,**" could equally well be translated "gate." It is used here to stand for any form of entrance or, more important, exit. The general idea is to have an escape route, a way out, or a backup plan should the trust be misplaced. Accordingly, a Klingon is generally apprehensive when someone says of a commitment or a plan, "**ngaQ lojmIt**" ("The door is locked"). The phrase "**ngaQ lojmIt**" is also sometimes heard in reference to a situation with an inevitable, unavoidable outcome.

The origin of the second proverb is unknown, but it seems to be related to an ancient political movement known as **ghIlaSnoS,** whose meaning has also been lost to obscurity.

When you begin a mission, remember Aktuh and Melota.

Qu' DataghDI' 'aqtu' mellota' je tIqaw.

Aktuh and Melota are the principal protagonists in a well-known Klingon opera titled *Aktuh and Melota.* The plot of the opera is so complex that the meaning of this commonly repeated maxim, which refers to it, has so far defied all attempts at interpretation.

ROBBIE ROBINSON

Assurances to the contrary, Worf is skeptical of the Yridian's information.

Don't trust Yridians who bring gifts.

nobmey qembogh yIrIDnganpu''e' yIvoqQo'.

Don't trust Ferengi who give back money.

Huch nobHa'bogh verenganpu''e' yIvoqQo'.

Yridians are known as traders of information—that is, buyers and sellers. So if a Yridian offers something at no cost—a gift—something is surely amiss.

Like the Klingons, the entrepreneurial Ferengi have a great many wise sayings, an important subset of which is known as the Ferengi Rules of Acquisition. The First Rule of Acquisition is "Once you have their money, you never give it back." Thus, Klingon thinking goes, if a Ferengi does return money, he is acting most suspiciously.

Both of these Klingon maxims embody the same general belief: Those who violate the rules of their own cultures and do not observe their own virtues are acting dishonorably and are not to be trusted.

He can sell ice on Rura Penthe.

rura' pente'Daq chuch ngevlaH ghaH.

Rura Penthe is a frozen asteroid used by the Klingons as a penal colony for enemies of the Empire. The expression is descriptive of somebody who can do most anything, even under adverse conditions.

Klingons look down on prisoners as having behaved dishonorably. If they had acted honorably, they would never have been captured in the first place. Although Klingon warriors fight to the death rather than take prisoners, there is a Klingon system of jurisprudence, and those who are found to have violated the rules of society are often punished by being forced to do particularly strenuous or distasteful work. Having such a system is actually seen as beneficial for Klingon society, since it provides a ready source of necessary labor. The prisoners on Rura Penthe, for example, mine dilithium, required for warp propulsion systems. Significantly, the penal colony houses no Klingon prisoners. A Klingon would never allow himself to be taken prisoner, not even by his own government.

Don't just aim; hit the target!

yIQeqQo' neH. DoS yIqIp!

This is another adage couched in the vocabulary of battle that actually has wider application. Klingons hold that there is no value in setting goals unless one achieves them. This attitude complements the belief, noted earlier (see page 135), that playing a game just for fun is an outlandish notion.

ROBBIE ROBINSON

Worf hears the clarion call of the Klingon warrior rise within him.

If a warrior does not fight, he does not breathe.

Suvbe'chugh SuvwI' tlhuHbe' SuvwI'.

Worf showed awareness of this aphorism when he explained to those in charge of space station Deep Space 9 that the accuracy of the Klingons' information that the Dominion was responsible for an uprising on the Cardassian homeworld was irrelevant. The Klingons were using it merely as a justification to go into battle. "There are many Klingons who say we have been at peace too long," he said. "Klingons are warriors, and warriors fight."

Perhaps Klingon General Chang was thinking of this expression as well when he told Kirk, "We need breathing room." Chang opposed the impending negotiations between the Empire and the Federation precisely because of the peace it would bring.

Deep Space Nine: The Way of the Warrior
Star Trek VI: The Undiscovered Country

ROBBIE ROBINSON

Gowron tries to convince his friend to join with him in the upcoming battle.

Hear the warrior cry out!

jach SuvwI' 'e' yIQoy!

Gowron referred to this well-known cry when he said to Worf, "Do you tremble and quake with fear at the approach of combat, hoping to *talk* your way out of a fight like a Human? Or do you hear the cry of the warrior calling you to battle, calling you to glory, like a Klingon? Are you one of us?" Worf later told Picard, "I *do* hear the cry of the warrior."

This exhortation resembles one cited earlier, "Listen to the voice of your blood" (see page 31). The two make the same point, but from different perspectives. To heed the cry of the warrior is to follow the dictates of the society; to listen to the voice of one's blood is to adhere to one's true nature. For Klingons, of course, both lead to the same result: living the life of a warrior.

The Next Generation: Redemption

Anger excites.

SeymoH QeH.

For Klingons, anger is definitely not a negative emotion. On the contrary, it can trigger acts of honor, energize battles, or prompt one to achieve one's goals. It provides motivation for further action and, since taking action is central to a Klingon's well-being, the overall effect is one of stimulation, elation, and excitement. One's outrage should not lead to recklessness, however, for careless action will interfere with one's ultimate success.

Federation diplomat Curzon Dax knew how Klingon anger could be channeled into action. On the first day of negotiations in the Korvat Colony, he walked out on a speech being delivered by Kang. Curzon knew that he had to get Kang very angry in order to create a bond between the Klingon and himself, and thereby ensure the success of his mission.

You pay attention to your Fek'lhr and I will pay attention to mine.

veqlarghlI' yIbuS 'ej veqlarghwI' vIbuS.

Fek'lhr is a mythical beast guarding Gre'thor, the place where the spirits of the dishonored dead go. Not really a devil (Kang once said that Klingons have no devil), it is still a being to be reckoned with. The phrase means that each individual has his own individual concerns, but it also is a warning to be aware of that part of each individual's being—the beast within, perhaps—that may entice one to stray onto a path leading to dishonor.

By blindfolding Ensign Sito (Shannon Fill), Worf hopes to teach her the importance of self-reliance.

Care about your students.

ghojwI'pu'lI' tISaH.

This bit of advice is actually—and probably intentionally—ambiguous. It can be interpreted to mean "care about your students' progress and welfare," but it can also mean "care about who your students are"—that is, impart knowledge only to those whom you trust.

To Klingons, knowledge and expertise are matters of pride. This includes both the understanding of history, rituals, and legends, and also the mastery of various practical techniques, such as those needed to be a successful warrior. Education and drilling continue throughout a Klingon's life. There are even some ritualized forms of practice, such as the **moQbara'**, a type of martial art, and the **qa'vaQ**, a hoop-and-stick maneuver that hones the skills of the hunt.

Complementing the value placed on learning is an emphasis on teaching, the recognition that, in order to continue as a culture, it is important to pass on expertise to future generations. At the same time, to grow as a culture, it is acknowledged that teachers will learn from their students, another reason to be sure that the student-teacher relationship is one of mutual trust and respect.

When an escaped prisoner looks for a guard, he always finds one.

'avwI' nejDI' narghta'bogh qama' reH 'avwI' Sambej.

This maxim carries a message similar to the Federation dictum "Don't go looking for trouble." It suggests that if one's being overcautious interferes with the task at hand, the task is doomed.

No enemy is boring.

Dal pagh jagh.

To be a warrior, one must have an opponent. Accordingly, antagonists or enemies are not deemed undesirable. At the very least, they are considered essential; in the case of truly worthy adversaries, they are admired. Engaging in battle with an enemy hones the warrior's skills and pushes him to achieve victory. To have a rich and fulfilling life, according to Klingon thinking, one must have an enemy.

Celebrating his birthday, Worf travels the gauntlet that marks the rite of the Age of Ascension.

Today I am a warrior.

DaHjaj SuvwI''e' jIH.

I must show you my heart.

tIqwIj Sa'angnIS.

I travel the river of blood.

'Iw bIQtIqDaq jIjaH.

Upon reaching a certain age, the Age of Ascension, a young Klingon undergoes a rite of passage symbolizing the attainment of a certain spiritual level. After intoning the three ancient and sacred phrases recorded above, the initiate, while walking along a path lined by painstik-wielding warriors, expresses his or her deepest feelings.

The Next Generation: The Icarus Factor

Ritual tools used in the Age of Ascension ceremony.

If you don't use the painstik, the child will never celebrate his Age of Ascension.

'oy'naQ Dalo'be'chugh not nenghep lop puq.

This is another way of saying that it is necessary to adhere strictly to the particulars of any procedure in order to achieve the desired goals. The proverb is phrased in terms of the details of Rite of Ascension, during which, as noted, warriors jab the Klingon youth with painstiks. If protocol is not followed—in this case, if painstiks are not used—the ceremony carries no import and the Age of Ascension has not been celebrated.

I am not a merry man.

loD Quch jIHbe'.

This is not a proverb or maxim of any kind, but rather an offhand remark made by Worf in reference to his nature. Though by itself of minor cultural importance, it nonetheless provides an example of Klingon introspection.

The Next Generation: Qpid

Don't catch any bugs.

ghewmey tISuqQo'.

The Klingon guard at listening post Morska found this advice funny. Klingon humor is difficult to understand, so there is no ready explanation as to why he was so amused.

Star Trek VI: The Undiscovered Country

Captured by Starfleet officers, Kor cares not for his own fate.

We succeed together in a greater whole.

wa' Dol nIvDaq matay'DI' maQap.

Kor said to Kirk and Spock, "Do you know why we are so strong? Because we are a unit. Each of us is part of a greater whole."

The Original Series: Errand of Mercy

Revered throughout the Empire, the image of Kahless is a constant in Klingon dwellings.

Destroying an empire to win a war is no victory, and ending a battle to save an empire is no defeat.

noH QapmeH wo' Qaw'lu'chugh yay chavbe'lu' 'ej wo' choqmeH may' DoHlu'chugh lujbe'lu'.

This is an ancient adage, originally voiced by Kahless himself.

Interestingly, when the Federation first started learning about Klingons, Kahless was considered to be no more than an evil conqueror. He had formed an empire of, in James Kirk's words, "conquered worlds." The Klingons, Kirk felt, "take what they want by arms and force." As part of their examination of the behavior of other life forms, the Excalbians staged a conflict between the forces of "good"—represented by Kirk, Spock, and the images of Abraham Lincoln and the Vulcan philosopher Surak—and those of "evil"—represented by, among others, the image of Kahless. The Excalbians formed their replica of Kahless on the basis of the Federation's conception of him. Therefore, they described him in terms fitting an oppressor: "the Klingon who set the pattern for his planet's tyrannies."

In time, and as more was learned about Klingon history and culture, the Federation's understanding of the role of Kahless in Klingon history changed. It is now known that Klingons consider him a great warrior who did indeed conquer other worlds, but united the Empire by giving the people the laws of honor which direct every Klingon's life.

Deep Space Nine: The Way of the Warrior
The Original Series: Friday's Child
The Original Series: The Savage Curtain

Have the courage to admit your mistakes.

Qaghmeyllj tIchID, yIyoH.

The Next Generation: Aquiel

Buy or die.

bIje'be'chugh vaj bIHegh.

This is a common saying among Klingon merchants, usually uttered when customers are in the store comparing products or sampling the available goods, but not purchasing anything. Tellingly, there is no known Klingon word for "browse," at least as applied to matters of commerce. Klingon shops do not have windows, but doing the in-store equivalent of window-shopping appears to be a bad idea.

Annotations used

Star Trek, The Original Series (logs of the *U.S.S. Enterprise*, NCC-1701, under the command of Captain James T. Kirk)

Star Trek II: The Wrath of Khan through *Star Trek VI: The Undiscovered Country* (logs of later voyages of the *U.S.S. Enterprise*, NCC-1701, under Kirk's command, as well as logs of a later *Enterprise*, NCC-1701-A)

Star Trek: The Next Generation (logs of the *U.S.S. Enterprise*, NCC-1701-D, under the command of Captain Jean-Luc Picard)

Star Trek: Deep Space Nine (logs of space station Deep Space 9 while under the command of Captain Benjamin Sisko)

Star Trek: Voyager (logs of *U.S.S. Voyager*, NCC-74656, under the command of Captain Kathryn Janeway)